HER DREAM HORSE?

Lisa's words turned into a yell of surprise as, without warning, Milky bucked, whirled, and tried to bolt back to the stable. Lisa fought for her balance. Milky broke into a gallop.

"Sit up!" Carole yelled. "Keep his head up!"

"Hang on!" Stevie hollered as Lisa and Milky disappeared into the pine woods. She and Carole quickly turned their horses and followed.

As soon as they reached the woods, they could see Lisa struggling with her mount. She was leaning back far enough that Milky couldn't unseat her, and she was pulling hard on the reins. Milky had slowed to a near walk. When he saw the other horses, he relaxed and allowed them to come up to him.

"Whoa." Lisa gradually let up on the reins. Milky walked forward as though he had done nothing wrong. But Lisa's heart was hammering, and her hands were shaking. "What was that about?" she asked her friends.

THE SADDLE CLUB

SCHOOLING
HORSE

BONNIE BRYANT

A SKYLARK BOOK
NEW YORK • TORONTO • LONDON • SYDNEY • AUCKLAND

RL 5, 009–012

SCHOOLING HORSE

A Bantam Skylark Book / November 1998

I would like to express my special thanks to Kimberly Brubaker Bradley for her help in the writing of this book.

1

"PRANCER!" LISA ATWOOD cried, her voice rising in frustration. She brought the elegant Thoroughbred mare she was riding from a canter to a walk, and then to a halt. Prancer threw up her head and squealed. "Stop that!" Lisa said. She used her legs and hands to make Prancer back up several strides. "Listen to me!" she told the mare.

"Circle her, Lisa. You've got the right idea. Get her attention, then ask her to canter again." Max Regnery, Lisa's riding instructor, spoke calmly, and Lisa felt a little ashamed of her outburst. Riding was difficult, as difficult as anything she had ever studied, but she was a straight-A student and she'd always learned quickly in the saddle, too. Prancer was one of Max's lesson horses, but Lisa loved her, and usually they made a good pair. Lisa thought they ought to be doing better than they were today.

But Prancer won't behave, she thought. *She knows how to act, and she's not doing it.* Lisa and her friends were in the middle of their usual Tuesday-afternoon group lesson. There were six horses in the ring. Every time one of the other horses came near Prancer, the mare squealed and tried to buck. She put her ears back and shook her head. Lisa was trying everything she knew to calm Prancer down, and nothing was working. Most of the time, when Prancer started a lesson fresh and excitable, it only took Lisa a few minutes to settle her into a learning frame of mind. Today it seemed as if the longer Lisa rode, the worse Prancer behaved.

"Come again with the canter," Max said. "Everyone, canter, please."

Lisa signaled Prancer to canter. Prancer dropped her head, cantered, then bucked. Lisa shouted at her.

"Press her forward, Lisa," Max said.

"I'm trying!" Lisa said.

"Everyone else halt," Max said. "Come into the center for a moment. Lisa, canter her hard. See if you can get her mind off her personal problems."

The five other students clustered in the center of the ring while Lisa galloped Prancer in circles around them. Stevie Lake maneuvered her mare, Belle, beside Carole Hanson's gelding, Starlight. Stevie, Carole, and Lisa were best friends.

"Wow," Stevie whispered sympathetically. "Prancer's giving Lisa a hard time. Think it's raccoons again?"

"What?" Carole asked, frowning at Stevie.

"I said, think it's raccoons again? You know, the raccoons that were stealing Prancer's grain." A short while before, a family of raccoons had taken up residence in the hayloft right above Prancer's stall, and Prancer had been upset for days before anyone figured out what was wrong. Stevie looked at Carole closely. "It was a joke, Carole. Or at least, sort of a joke." Stevie was famous for her practical—and impractical—jokes.

"Okay," Carole said. She gave her horse an absent-minded pat and looked across the arena. Stevie was concerned. All three friends were horse-crazy, but Carole was the horse-craziest. Usually she couldn't keep her mind on anything but horses, but today her attention seemed to be somewhere else. Thinking back, Stevie realized that Carole hadn't looked happy once that afternoon.

Stevie studied Starlight closely, but the horse seemed in perfect health. He was doing well in the lesson, too. "What's wrong?" Stevie asked Carole. "Are you feeling okay?"

Carole shook her head, and Stevie was amazed to see tears well up in her eyes. Carole pressed her lips together. "I can't talk about it," she whispered at last. "Not during the lesson."

"Okay," Stevie whispered back. "Afterward, then." The three friends had a rule that they always, no matter what, helped each other out. That and being incurably

3

horse-crazy were the only two requirements for member-ship in the club they'd formed, The Saddle Club. In truth, Stevie thought as she stroked Belle's neck and watched Lisa canter by, they were all as friend-crazy as they were horse-crazy. As much as Stevie cared for Belle, she cared for her friends more.

On the rail Prancer again tried to buck. "Oh!" Lisa said. Her face was red from exertion, and she was breath-ing hard.

"Another lap," Max said. "She's starting to settle down."

"She doesn't feel settled down," Lisa said.

Max grinned. "More settled, then," he said. "This may be as good as she gets today. Are you okay, Lisa?"

"I'm not scared," Lisa said. "But I'm annoyed."

"Don't let yourself get too frustrated. None of this is your fault."

Easy for Max to say, Lisa thought resentfully. *If he were sitting on this horse, he might wonder why she wasn't listening or behaving at all.* She quickly looked sideways at Stevie and Carole, who were sitting in the middle of the ring, waiting for her to get Prancer back under control. *Wait-ing*, Lisa thought with a spurt of resentment she didn't usually feel toward her two best friends, *on their* own *horses.*

When Lisa had first started riding, her parents had of-fered to buy her a horse and had even taken her to look at a few. But even though Lisa hadn't been riding long, she'd ridden long enough to realize how much she still didn't know. Back then she hadn't been ready for her own horse. She'd still been a beginner, and the safe, easy sort of beginner horse she would have needed then, she would have outgrown by now. Plus, back then she'd had no idea how to care for a horse. So even though she wanted one very badly, she'd told her parents not to buy her one.

Now Lisa was starting to feel ready for a horse of her own. She was never jealous of Stevie and Carole—after all, they'd been riding much longer than she had—but sometimes she envied the special relationships they had with Belle and Starlight. Even though she rode Prancer several times a week, it wasn't the same. Especially today.

"What do you think's gotten into Prancer?" Stevie asked Carole. She was starting to get bored with sitting still.

Carole watched Lisa and Prancer make another half circuit of the ring. "I think she's in heat," Carole said.

"Oh!" Stevie thought for a moment. "I bet you're right. She's acting pretty awful, though, even with that as an excuse." Mares often seemed skittish and grouchy when they were in heat. It was one reason many riders preferred geldings.

"It's cold out, too," Carole said. "And Lisa didn't ride yesterday, so Prancer might not have gotten out."

Stevie nodded. "Poor Lisa."

On the rail, Prancer suddenly slowed to a trot. Lisa, her legs aching, sighed in relief. "Canter her," Max commanded. "Make her canter another lap, then ask her to trot."

5

Lisa nodded, though it took all her strength to press Prancer forward again. Prancer had to trot when Lisa wanted her to, not when Prancer wanted to. They cantered another lap, then Lisa slowed her to a trot, nearly gasping from relief. "I don't know if it's settled Prancer down," she told Max, "but it's settled me down, that's for sure."

"You're doing fine," Max said with a smile. "Horses have bad days, just like people. You're coping, Lisa."

"I can always cope," Lisa said. "But she's driving me crazy."

Max nodded sympathetically. One of the many things Lisa appreciated about him was that he always seemed to understand his students' troubles. "Why don't you come see me in the office after the lesson?" he suggested. "We can talk about how to handle this."

"Thanks, Max," Lisa said gratefully.

Max started the lesson up again, and in a few minutes he had them all jumping a course of fences. This was where Starlight and Carole usually shined—they loved jumping more than anything else. Today, however, something was missing. Starlight was approaching the fences correctly, but he didn't seem to be jumping with enthusiasm, and Carole wasn't smiling.

"What's with Starlight?" Lisa hissed to Stevie as they waited their turns to jump.

"He's just picking up on Carole's mood," Stevie told her friend. "She's upset about something. She said she'd tell us later."

Lisa nodded. She watched with concern as Starlight added a stride in front of the big rolltop jump, then lurched over it. Normally Starlight relished jumping. But she could see that Carole wasn't riding him well. For Carole to look like that, Lisa decided, she must really be upset.

Suddenly Prancer threw her head up. She craned her neck around to get a closer look at whatever had caught her attention. Lisa sighed. It was nothing—just a horse trailer pulling into the driveway. Prancer was being so annoying!

Max looked over at the horse trailer, too. "That's enough of a lesson for today," he told the students. "Cool your horses out while I deal with our new arrival. Lisa, don't forget to come talk to me later."

"Did you buy a new horse, Max?" Stevie asked.

"Sort of. This horse is here on trial." Max let himself out of the ring and walked toward the trailer.

"What does that mean?" Stevie asked her friends.

"It means the horse might stay, and it might not," Carole said.

"No kidding," Stevie said. "I just meant, why did Max say it that way? Usually when we get a new horse, either it's a boarder belonging to someone else or Max has already bought it."

"I don't know," Carole said. "Maybe there's something special about this horse."

Lisa watched as the man who had driven the truck backed the horse carefully out of the trailer. "It looks like

7

something special," she said. The horse was a nearly white gray with a fine, intelligent-looking face and long, slender legs. "It looks like a Thoroughbred."

The horse pricked its ears and studied its new surroundings curiously. Max walked up to it and held out his hand. The horse laid its ears back and danced sideways, away from Max. The other man spoke to it, and the horse stood still.

Carole nodded. "I bet you're right. I wonder if it's a gelding or a mare. I wonder what its name is."

"Max will tell us," Stevie said. "But right now we want you to tell us what's wrong."

Carole nodded. "Inside the barn," she said.

Stevie and Lisa dealt with their horses quickly, then met just outside Starlight's stall. Inside, Carole had taken off Starlight's saddle but not his bridle. She was standing with her arms around his neck and her face buried in his mane. Her shoulders were quivering.

"Carole!" Stevie gave her a hug. "Whatever it is, we'll help."

Carole took a step backward and brushed the few remaining tears from her eyes. "I know," she said. "Thanks—I can use your help, for sure. And it helps to have a horse to hug. It's French."

"Your horse is French?" Stevie asked. That didn't sound right.

Carole laughed shakily. "No. My problem is French. French class."

"Ah," Stevie said. "But I thought you said you liked

8

that class." Stevie went to Fenton Hall, a private school, so she never had the same teachers as Lisa and Carole, who went to Willow Creek's public school.

"I do," Carole said. "But I'm *failing.*"

"Failing? You can't be failing. Carole, that's ridiculous." Lisa frowned. Carole was smart, and even though she was sometimes absentminded, she usually did well in school. Lisa tried to remember what she'd heard about the introductory French classes at school. She was a year ahead of Carole, but she was taking Spanish, not French.

"I failed today," Carole said. She kicked at the loose straw in Starlight's stall. "We had another oral presentation—we just started those, but we're going to have two or three a week from now on—and I failed it. I actually got an F." Her voice trembled.

"I've actually gotten an F one or two times before," Stevie said. "It wasn't fun, but it wasn't the end of the world."

"But Stevie, I was trying!" Carole said. "I studied hard!"

"Oh," Stevie said. "Ouch. That's different."

"How long has this been a problem?" Lisa asked. "Why didn't you tell us before?"

Carole unbuckled Starlight's bridle and smoothed his forelock. "It just started," she said. "See, I like French, and I like my teacher, and when school began he just had us all speaking in a group. He'd tell us sounds or words, and the whole class would recite them in unison. That was okay. And I'm doing fine in the written and listening parts. But now we have to get up in front of the class and speak it all by ourselves, and I just can't. My voice doesn't make those sounds. Last week I got a C in my first dialogue and a D in my second. I practiced all evening for this one, and then I couldn't sleep . . . and then I got an F."

Lisa patted Carole's arm. "That must have felt horrible," she said. "But it is something we can help you with. We don't know French—"

"I can help with Latin," Stevie suggested. "*Meus equus est delicia nominatus Belle*. That's Latin for, 'My horse is a sweetheart named Belle.' My Latin teacher helped me translate it. It's actually a difficult translation, see, because—"

Lisa gave Stevie a look. Sometimes Stevie didn't know when to be quiet.

"Sorry," Stevie said, subsiding quickly. "But Lisa's right. We'll find a way to help."

"Thanks," Carole said. "I was afraid you guys would think I was stupid. You can't imagine how awful it feels to try and try to learn something and still not be able to. When I did my dialogue today, three people laughed. I felt so humiliated."

"We'll never laugh," Stevie said. "You know that."

Carole nodded. "Yes, I do. And that does help."

"I felt pretty stupid today, too," Lisa said. "Did you see me and Prancer? I could not get her under control."

"I think she's in heat," Carole said.

"I do, too," Lisa said. "Even so, she was ridiculous."

"Let's go see Max about it," Stevie suggested. "Then, Carole, we'll talk tonight about your French problem. We'll brainstorm."

They walked into the office. "Hey, Max," Stevie said, "what's the name of the new horse?"

Max smiled. "Well," he said, "for now he's called Au Lait, but I have to say I don't much like the name."

"Olé?" Carole asked. "Like what they say in bullfights?"

"No, Au Lait," Max said. He wrote it out on the office chalkboard. "It's French for 'with milk.' I guess because of his color."

Carole shook her head. "I should have taken Spanish."

"Lisa," Max asked, "would you like to ride someone else for a little while?"

Lisa sat down. "Do you really think we were that bad?" she asked.

"No," Max said. "In fact, I think you handled a difficult situation pretty well. You know Prancer's in heat?"

Lisa nodded.

"But you seemed pretty upset about her behavior," Max continued. "You got frustrated a little more quickly than you usually do."

"She was bugging me," Lisa said. "I don't know why."

"So why don't you ride another horse for a week or so?" Max suggested. "You and Prancer can both have a rest from each other, and you'll learn some different things by riding a different horse."

Lisa thought about his suggestion. In a way it made her feel better, but in a way it made her feel worse. "Wouldn't I be giving up on Prancer?" she asked.

"Of course not," Max said. "It would just be a little vacation, and you could ride her again whenever you wanted to. I'd like to say you could ride Derby, but you know Mrs. Bradley's planning to take him in a show next month."

"Yes." Lisa sighed. She'd ridden Derby over the summer and liked him quite a lot. Mrs. Bradley was an older woman who'd recently started riding at the barn.

"It's her first show, and she's nervous about it," Max explained. "She's been riding Derby every day. I'd like her to be able to keep doing that. But you could take Topside, if you want."

"He's a lot of fun, Lisa," Stevie said. Topside was Stevie's old favorite.

"Maybe," Lisa said. "Can I let you know tomorrow?"

"Of course," Max said. "And don't let yourself get too discouraged. Bright times are ahead."

MAX CAN SAY *what he wants*, Lisa thought as she quietly let herself into her house. *I still feel lousy.*

"Of course, Max," Lisa heard her mother say. "I don't want her finding out until everything is settled." Lisa's ears pricked up. She set her backpack on the floor very quietly and crept down the hall. Why was her mother talking to Max? Lisa peeked into the kitchen.

Her mother was on the phone. "The most important

thing is that it suits Lisa," Mrs. Atwood said firmly. "I really don't want to make a mistake about this. Thank you, Max, I knew you'd understand." She hung up.

"Hi, Mom," Lisa said, walking into the room. "Who were you talking to?"

Mrs. Atwood spun around. "Oh . . . nobody," she said. "Nobody important. How was your day?"

"Nobody important" was named Max. Lisa went up to her room, wondering what her mother was keeping secret, and why.

"Aujourd'hui," Carole said. "That is a word. Can you believe it? I can't believe it. I certainly can't pronounce it."

"It sounded fine to us," Stevie said. The Saddle Club was having a three-way phone conversation after dinner that evening. The phones at Stevie's house had all the latest gadgets, and she usually called her friends every night.

"Well, it's not." Carole sounded ready to spit. "I've heard the way it's supposed to be pronounced, and trust me, I'm not even close. The middle is supposed to kind of slurp, like you're swallowing it up, only you roll the r, and the end is supposed to be almost a whistle."

"See," Lisa said, "you know exactly what you're supposed to be doing. You must be paying close attention."

"It's no help to know what I'm supposed to be doing if I can't do it," Carole said. "I can't roll my rs or make that little slurp. I tried it so much tonight my dad thought I had indigestion."

"They shouldn't have hard words like that in introductory French," Stevie said. "It's not fair."

"It means 'today,' " Carole said. "That's all it means."

"Oh," said Stevie.

"I've got a whole dialogue to learn, and I can't pronounce any of it. Listen to this." Carole read several lines into the phone.

"Sounds like French to me," Stevie said.

"It wouldn't if you knew anything about French," Carole said.

"Which we don't," Lisa reminded her. "We're sorry, Carole, but we don't know what sounds correct and what doesn't. That's probably not something we can help you with."

"I know," Carole said. "I'm sorry, too; I don't mean to be rude. But I don't know what to do. My dad learned two languages in the Marine Corps, and do you know what they are? Vietnamese and Mandarin! What use is that? And my mom was actually a French major in college. It seems so unfair." Carole's mother had died several years before. "I just don't know what I'm going to do!" Carole's voice rose to a tone of despair.

"I know it must be really unpleasant for you to get an

15

F," Stevie said, "and I understand how awful it would be to get up in front of your class and do poorly. But I think you're letting yourself get a little too upset. It's just one part of one class."

"Except that it's a very important part," Carole replied. "My teacher says we have to be able to speak French at level one in order to go on to level two next year. He says if we fail the oral part of the class, we fail the whole class."

"Oh no," Lisa said. "You don't want to fail."

"I *can't* fail," Carole said. "Think about it! What would Max do?"

For a moment there was complete silence on all three ends of the phone. "Wow," Stevie whispered at last. "I never thought of that."

"Max's academic policy," Lisa said.

"That's right," Carole said.

Max took a very strict line with his young riders at Pine Hollow. Schoolwork always had to come before riding. Anyone who got less than a C in any subject wasn't allowed to ride at the barn until the grade had improved.

"He wouldn't kick you out of the barn," Lisa said. "Not you, Carole. He couldn't."

"He'd have to," Carole said. "Max always follows his own rules. I'd have to move Starlight to another stable. . . . I wouldn't be able to ride with you guys. . . . I couldn't belong to Horse Wise. . . ." Her voice trailed off in misery.

"We'll never let that happen," Stevie promised.

16

"Never," Lisa said. She couldn't imagine Pine Hollow without Carole. "There's got to be something we can do to help."

"Maybe you could figure out a way to relate French to horses," Stevie suggested. "You never have any problem learning anything about horses." Carole knew more obscure horse facts than anyone else Stevie'd ever met.

"Horses don't speak French," Carole said.

"Or English," Lisa added. Max reminded them of that every time he caught them chatting to their mounts.

"But they have a language," Stevie protested. "The way they move their ears and snort and stuff."

"True, but hardly useful," Carole said. "I've learned to communicate with Starlight just fine, and it didn't require that I learn to whinny. Good thing, too. I probably couldn't pronounce that right, either."

"You know," said Lisa, who had been thinking seriously about Carole's problem while Stevie blathered on about horses, "maybe you should use a tape recorder. In Spanish class, we always listen to a tape of the dialogues we have to say. Do you do that?"

"Sure," said Carole. "That's how we know how they're supposed to sound."

"Maybe you could make yourself a copy of the class tapes," Lisa said. "Then you could bring it home and listen to it over and over. And you could tape yourself saying the dialogues and find out exactly what you're doing wrong. It would be a lot of work—"

"But it really might help," Carole said with a burst of

enthusiasm. "Thank you, Lisa. That's a great idea. I'm sure Mr. Norris would let me copy the tapes."

"And have confidence in yourself," Stevie advised. "You know you can do anything you set your mind to."

"I thought I could," Carole said. "After today I'm beginning to doubt it."

"Keep trying," Stevie said. "Whenever you get discouraged, call us."

"Thanks," Carole said. "I really appreciate it."

Lisa twirled the phone cord in her fingers. "I've got to tell you about something I overheard this afternoon," she said. "I don't have any idea what it means, but I'm dying to figure it out." She related what she'd heard her mother say.

"She really said 'Max'?" Stevie asked. "Are you sure she was talking to Max?"

"I guess I don't know for sure that she was talking to *our* Max," Lisa admitted. "But she definitely said 'Max.' If she weren't talking to our Max, why wouldn't she have answered when I asked her who it was? Why wouldn't she have just said, 'Oh, I was talking to Max the furniture repairman about getting that sofa leg fixed'? I'm pretty sure my mom and Max have some kind of secret between them."

"Cool," said Stevie. "Whatever it is, it can't be bad."

"I don't think so, either," Lisa admitted. "If Max or my mother were upset with me, I'd know about it. So it must be something good. And it's something my mom wants to be sure is exactly right—exactly right for me."

"A horse," Carole said. "They're getting you a horse! Max has found one, but they want to be sure it's right for you."

"That's the only thing I could think of," Lisa confessed. She felt so excited that she laughed out loud. "You know, I've really been wanting my own horse lately—I think I'm ready for one now—and when I heard Mom say that, I thought *horse* right away. But I was worried that I only thought it because I wanted it so badly."

"No, it makes perfect sense," Stevie said. "Wow! Wouldn't that be cool?"

"It would be wonderful," Carole said. "Lisa, we're so happy for you."

"That'll put an end to your problems with Prancer," Stevie said.

"Oh." In her excitement, Lisa had already dismissed their difficult lesson from her mind. "I love Prancer, even when she's driving me crazy. But I can't wait to see this horse Max has found for me. Just think—I'll be able to have the kind of relationship you guys have with your horses."

"It'll be entirely yours," Carole said. "You'll be able to teach it everything."

Lisa sighed in delight. "I wonder what color it will be. Since Belle and Starlight are both bays—"

"Gray," Stevie cut in.

"You think gray? I know color's not that important, but wouldn't it be fun if we all matched?"

"I'm not suggesting you look for a gray horse," Stevie said. "I'm saying, maybe it *is* a gray horse. Maybe we've already seen it. Maybe it's that horse that came to the stable today."

"Au Lait," Lisa said, remembering. "Gosh. I think he was a Thoroughbred. Do you think he could be the one?"

"It makes sense," Stevie argued. "Why else would Max have said he was at the stable on trial? Your parents want to see if he'll work out before they buy him."

"And why else would Max have said you should take a break from Prancer?" Carole added. "He's never said that before."

Lisa remembered how elegant Au Lait had looked, stepping off the trailer and looking around Pine Hollow with a fine, aristocratic eye. He was a sensitive horse, like Prancer—she remembered how he'd flinched away from Max's outstretched hand. But Lisa was used to riding sensitive horses. She would do well with him.

A great bubble of delight welled up inside Lisa's chest. Stevie and Carole were right. It made perfect sense that the new horse was there for her to try. Her parents must not want her to know until the decision was final—they wouldn't want to disappoint her if the horse didn't work out. But Lisa knew he would. He was beautiful, and she would love him.

"My own horse," she said. "Au Lait." She loved the

sound of the words. *My own horse*, she repeated to herself. *Mine*.

"Please, can't you call him something else?" Carole pleaded. "I'd like Pine Hollow to be one place where I could forget about my French class."

"How about Milky?" Stevie suggested. "Max said that's what his name means."

"For now that would be okay," Lisa said. "But later I'm going to think of a better name."

"Milky Way," said Stevie.

"Maybe," Lisa said. "I don't think I want my horse named after a candy bar. I'll think of something good, but it will probably take me a little while."

"Remember how long it took Stevie to name Belle?" Carole said.

"Remember all the weird names I considered?" Stevie laughed. "I'm still grateful I didn't go with Tabriz."

"So are we," Carole assured her.

WHEN LISA HUNG up the phone she did a little dance of happiness around the room. Her own horse! She pictured herself at next summer's Briarwood Horse Show, riding her fine gray gelding over jump after jump, elegant, in perfect form. She'd give Carole and Starlight a run for their money.

How wonderful that her parents understood. They must have realized that this was the right time for her to own a horse. They must have been paying attention all along.

Lisa hugged herself, then did a pirouette on the soft carpet. Her own horse! Her own horse to train and love forever—just like Stevie and Carole! She tried to recall everything she could about Milky—how he'd moved when he stepped off the trailer, how he'd looked around, inspecting his new home. He would like Pine Hollow, Lisa knew. He'd love her the way Starlight loved Carole, the way Belle loved Stevie. She'd ride him every day.

Lisa tried to do her homework but found it impossible to concentrate on any subject but Milky. Even when she finally went to sleep, she saw herself riding a gray horse in her dreams.

3

AFTER SCHOOL THE next day, Lisa set out for Pine Hollow with a light heart. Even the gloomy November weather couldn't dampen her spirits. She had a horse. No, she corrected herself, she was going to have a horse. Soon she would have a horse. She had spent half the school day trying to think of a new name for Au Lait—Milky—and half drawing pictures of him in the margins of her notebooks.

"Hey, Carole," she'd said, catching up to her friend when the last bell for the day had finally rung, "what do you think of Snowdrop?"

Carole had known immediately what Lisa meant. She'd wrinkled her nose. "Good for a pony," she'd said. "But your boy is a little too grown up for a name like that."

"True." Lisa smiled to think of Milky as a grown-up horse. *My boy*, she thought. She liked the sound of that. "You're coming to Pine Hollow today, aren't you?" she asked.

Carole made a face. "As soon as I can," she said. "I've got to go make copies of those French tapes now. My teacher did think it was a good idea."

"Great," Lisa said. "Later, if you want, I can help you tape yourself. Or listen to them with you, or whatever else I can do."

"Thanks." Carole looked at Lisa's happy face and smiled. "I bet you can't wait to see that horse."

"I can't," Lisa admitted. "I've been thinking about him all day, but you know, I didn't pay him much attention yesterday. I can't really remember if he had any markings or anything."

"You'll make up for that today," Carole had said.

"That's for sure," Lisa had said. "I'll see you at the barn—I know I'll still be there when you arrive."

Now Lisa shoved her backpack higher onto her shoulder and walked a little faster. It was a quick walk between school and Pine Hollow—especially quick if you were eager to see a particular horse. Lisa wondered what Max would be doing with Milky. She hoped he would let her ride him right away.

Lisa walked up the drive. She could see Max teaching a class of younger riders, whose school let out earlier than the junior high. Lisa thought she saw a tall gray horse among those being used for the lesson. She hurried for-

ward, hoping it was Milky—and saw little Jessica Adler
lying in a heap on the ground. Max was kneeling in the
dirt beside her, patting her shoulder while she sobbed. A
gray horse—it was Milky, Lisa realized with dismay—galloped past the other kids with his saddle empty, reins and
stirrups flying.

Lisa ran the last few steps to the arena fence. Red, Pine
Hollow's head stable hand, was standing by the gate.
"What happened?" Lisa asked. "Is Jessica okay?"

Red nodded. "She's mad and she's scared," he said.
"She isn't hurt."

Lisa drew a deep breath. "Good. Did she do something
to Milky, or did Milky do something to her?" All riders
occasionally fell off. Sometimes it was the horse's fault,
sometimes it was the rider's fault, and sometimes it just
happened.

"Milky?" Red said. "You mean that Au Lait?" He pronounced it *Ow Late*. Lisa smiled and nodded. Carole
wasn't the only person at the stable who couldn't speak
French.

"Hard to tell," Red said. "The horse was acting up
a bit. He seemed okay earlier, though, when I rode
him."

"You rode him? What was he like?" Lisa watched Max
help Jessica to her feet. He bent his head low and spoke
soothingly to the little girl.

"Fine," Red said. "Real well trained, knows everything
you want him to know. Max tried him, too, and seemed
to like him."

"Oh, good." Lisa sighed with relief. Probably Jessica had just lost her balance.

"He kept refusing in front of the fences for Jessica, though," Red continued with a shake of his head. "I don't understand it, because it sure wasn't how he acted before."

"He's probably not used to our jumps yet," Lisa said. "And he might not be used to sharing the ring with other horses, particularly unfamiliar horses. He's probably nervous." *Poor Milky,* she thought. *He needs to be ridden by someone who understands.*

"Red," Max called from the center of the ring, "can you help Jessica saddle Penny fast? She's going to finish the lesson with her. I want her to have a chance at these fences again so she can get her confidence back." Penny was a trustworthy old pony. Lisa thought she was much more Jessica's style than a Thoroughbred like Milky.

"Right on it," Red said. "Come on, Jessica."

Max was holding Milky by the reins in the center of the ring. "You're next, May," he called to one of the other kids in the lesson.

"Should I take Milky inside for you, Max?" Lisa volunteered. "I can untack him and put him away." *A good grooming and lots of carrots,* she thought. *That would make Milky feel better.*

Max looked confused. "Milky?"

"The horse," Lisa said, pointing.

"Oh—Oh, hey, good name. Better than Au Lait, anyway." Max grinned at her. "Tell you what, Lisa, you could do me a bigger favor right now. I don't want Au—er, Milky—learning that when he tosses a rider over a fence, he gets to go back to his stall and have a nice rest and dinner. Would you mind riding him in the ring here while I finish the lesson? If you feel up to some jumps with him, so much the better."

Lisa smiled to herself at the way Max made having her ride Milky sound like something he'd just thought of. She guessed that he and her mother really wanted the truth about Milky to stay a secret for now. Lisa was willing to play along. And she realized that Max was right—Milky didn't need treats. He needed to learn what was expected of him. *From now on,* Lisa thought, *I'm going to be the one responsible for his training.* It gave her a thrill.

"Sure," she said. "I'll get changed and be right out."

In a minute Lisa was back, buckling the strap to her hard hat. Jessica was trotting Penny in circles to warm her up while Nicholas took a turn over the jumps. "Watch out for him," Jessica warned Lisa. "He's mean."

Lisa smiled at the little girl. "He's new here," she said gently. "I'm sorry he dumped you, but I'm sure he's just nervous and scared."

Jessica shook her head. "He's nasty," she said. "I'm never riding him again."

That's right, you aren't, Lisa thought as she checked Milky's girth. *Because he's going to be my horse. Once he's officially mine, no one else is ever going to ride him again unless I say so.* She patted Milky's white neck, gathered the reins, and mounted.

At first Milky seemed upset. He ground his teeth over the bit, swished his tail angrily, tossed his head down, and bucked. Lisa, still in the process of finding her seat, nearly came off, but she threw her weight back and yanked on Milky's head. He stopped bucking and walked forward. "That's it," Lisa said. "Good boy." She shoved her heels down.

"Trot him back and forth over the cross rail until you feel comfortable with him," Max said. "Then you can have a go at the wall where he threw Jessica."

The wall was a little one, only about eighteen inches high, and Max usually put a rail or two over it to make it higher. Now he carefully lowered the rails. Lisa trotted Milky over the cross rail several times, then headed him toward the wall. She tightened her legs around his barrel and tried to give him firm, no-nonsense jump-the-fence signals. Milky trotted smartly up to the fence, lifted his forelegs to jump, and then slammed them back down to the ground. Lisa barely managed to keep herself from flying over his head.

"Good job," Max said. "That was a nasty stop."

Lisa was somewhat startled by her near fall. She'd been certain that Milky was going to jump the fence. "He must be pretty nervous," she said.

"Peanuts," Max said. "He jumped it three or four times for me without acting stupid. I know he can do it."

Lisa nodded. She rode at the wall a second time with all the more determination. She kept her weight well back in the saddle and drove Milky forward with her heels. This time, instead of stopping, Milky left the ground early, jumping the fence with such a huge leap that Lisa nearly fell off him backward.

"Next time, grab his mane," Max said.

Lisa blushed. She'd been riding Milky for exactly five minutes and had already almost fallen off three times. "Okay," she said. Unlike people, horses don't have nerves in the roots of their hair. Grabbing the horse's mane wouldn't hurt it at all. "Sorry."

"Don't feel bad," Max said. "You're doing fine with him. Ride him around for a few minutes while I give the class another course. Then you can try the wall again."

Lisa trotted and cantered Milky in circles. Once he tried to buck again, and once he aimed a kick at Jasmine's pony, but when he was paying attention to Lisa he moved well. She liked his fast trot and the way he picked his head up when he cantered. She worked him for a long time, trying to get him to settle down and keeping him out of the way of the other riders in the ring. It wasn't easy—Milky still seemed upset about something—but Lisa persevered gladly. In a few months, she'd have Milky jumping as well as Belle and Starlight.

Carole and Stevie arrived at the stables just as Max was ready to have Lisa start jumping again. Lisa waved to them, then turned her attention back to Milky and the troublesome wall. This time Milky jumped it as calmly as if it had never bothered him before. "Good boy!" Lisa cried. She leaned forward to pat Milky's neck. Milky put his ears back and bucked. Lisa hung off-balance for a moment, then jerked herself back into the saddle. Milky rounded the corner at a gallop.

Lisa grinned. That fence had been so much better! She pulled on the reins to slow Milky down. "Try the white gate next," Max said. "Is he upsetting you?"

"No," Lisa said. "He's fabulous!" She turned Milky toward the white gate. Milky eyed it, sped up, then at the last moment came to a stop. Lisa popped him on the backside with her crop. Milky bunched himself together and jumped at the last possible moment, but Lisa had grabbed a double handful of mane, and she stayed in the saddle. "Good boy!" she cried.

Carole saw Max raise a skeptical eyebrow at Lisa's comments. She shook her head in agreement. "I don't know that I'd call him good," she whispered to Stevie. "Awful is more like it."

Stevie nodded. "He's jumping terribly," she said. "Do you think Lisa doesn't notice?"

"I think Lisa's glad he's jumping at all," Carole said. "And I guess that's saying something. I mean, he just got here and all." Carole hated to criticize Lisa's new horse. Not every horse could be like Starlight.

"Yeah," Stevie said. "You know, maybe he hasn't had much experience. Or maybe he's just a nervous type of horse. It might take him a while to get used to Pine Hollow."

"And to Lisa," Carole agreed. It made her happy to think of a logical reason why the horse was acting poorly. In the ring now he was cantering too fast. When Lisa pulled on the reins to slow him down, he put his ears back and swished his tail angrily. Carole shook her head. She really hated to sound rude, but . . . "Does he look like Lisa's type of horse to you?" she asked Stevie.

"I was just thinking that he doesn't," Stevie admitted. "I mean, probably he'll get a lot better once he's been settled here awhile, and Max is a really good trainer, but . . ." She found it hard to say exactly what she meant. Milky didn't impress her, but she couldn't say why he didn't.

"Prancer's kind of excitable," Carole said, "but most of the time she tries hard to please Lisa. This horse . . ." Like Stevie, Carole couldn't quite put what she meant into words. Milky didn't look like a friendly horse, and she thought Lisa ought to have a friendly horse. But she was afraid that was a silly thing to say.

Lisa trotted Milky up to her two friends. "What do you think?" she asked them, her eyes aglow. "Isn't he gorgeous?"

"He's very handsome," Carole said honestly.

"He needs to behave better," Lisa said. "But he got a lot better in just a little while here. I can't wait to see what a week or two will do." She leaned over to stroke Milky's neck. "I just love him," she admitted in a whisper. "I mean, thinking about having him for my own . . ." She shrugged and grinned at her friends.

"It's the best feeling in the world," Stevie said. She remembered the day she got Belle. "Lisa, we're so happy for you. And we'll help you train him, you know that."

Max finished talking to the younger riders and walked over to The Saddle Club. "So, you weren't too upset by him?" he asked Lisa.

Lisa grinned. "No. He really got a lot better. And he's got so much talent, Max, once he gets over his nervousness."

Max looked the gray horse up and down. "He is beautiful," he said. "I'm glad he didn't frighten you, Lisa. He didn't act much better with you than he did with Jessica, but you didn't let it rattle you." Max shook his head. "He was a lot better this morning, or I wouldn't have let Jessica on him in the first place."

"I really like him," Lisa assured Max. "I'd love to keep riding him."

"Okay," Max said. "If you want, you can ride him the way you would normally ride Prancer."

Lisa, Stevie, and Carole all grinned at each other. Max was certainly good at keeping Mrs. Atwood's secret.

"That would be super," Lisa said.

Max held up his hand. "One thing, Lisa. We don't know this horse very well. I want you to report to me with any problem you have. *Any* little thing. Understood?"

"Of course," Lisa said. She reached down to pat Milky again. One thing Lisa knew for sure. She might ask Max for help training Milky, but she certainly wasn't going to complain herself out of owning a horse.

ON FRIDAY AFTER school Carole threw her backpack into her cubby at Pine Hollow with undisguised relief. "It's the weekend," she said to Stevie and Lisa, who were changing into their riding clothes.

"We know that," Stevie answered with a grin.

"How was your French class?" Lisa asked. Carole had had a dialogue due that day. Judging from her smile, Lisa guessed it had gone well. "Did having the tapes help?"

Carole stretched her arms over her head, then reached for her old baggy sweatshirt to cover her school blouse. "They're helping," she said. "But what really made today fantastic was the surprise assembly this afternoon."

Lisa shook her head. "Fantastic? That was so boring." It had been about some fund-raiser to upgrade the computer

33

lab. Lisa had spent the hour drawing pictures of Milky in her science notebook. "You're not seriously interested in selling coupon books, are you?"

Carole grinned. "No—but because of the assembly, they canceled French class! My dialogue won't be until Monday!"

Lisa laughed. Stevie said, "That's great. You'll be really good at it by then."

"I hope so," Carole said. "You don't mind if I bring my tape recorder to the sleepover, do you?" They were all spending the night at Stevie's house.

"Of course not," Stevie said. "We'll listen and see if we can help you."

"I feel so good!" Carole exclaimed. She pulled on her boots. "Even though I've studied a lot, and I can tell that I'm improving, I was really dreading that class. Let's take a trail ride. What do you think?" She looked out the window of the locker room. The day before, it had rained. "I think it's been windy enough today to dry the trails."

"Sounds great," Stevie said. "I can tell Belle is sick of being cooped up in a ring. Lisa?"

Lisa shrugged. "Sure. Only . . . it'll be Milky's first trail ride. I mean, his first one here. I don't know how much he's been ridden on trails, if at all. He might get kind of nervous."

"We'll stick to a slow walk," Carole said. "We won't go any faster unless you want to. Belle and Starlight will give him good examples. He'll be okay." She could see that Lisa was also a little nervous about going on a trail ride.

Milky would probably be fine, but Lisa usually took a while to adjust to change. Carole guessed it was difficult for her, riding a different horse than Prancer.

"Thanks," Lisa said. Cautiously she added, "It should be fun." *If only Milky behaves*, she said to herself. She wondered why she was feeling so apprehensive about riding Milky outside the safe confines of the ring. After all, she went on trail rides with Prancer all the time and loved them, and so far Milky hadn't behaved too badly.

Not too badly, Lisa repeated to herself as she got Milky's saddle out of the tack room and went to get him ready to ride. *Not too badly, but not too well, either.* She stopped outside Milky's stall. "Hello, boy!" she said in her most cheerful voice. Milky raised his head from the pile of hay he was eating and looked at her calmly. He didn't seem glad to see her—why should he, after all? He hardly knew her.

But he didn't seem to want to know her. That, Lisa thought, was part of the problem. She wasn't sure what the rest of the problem was. In fact, she couldn't say for sure that there *was* a problem. She only knew that somehow the last few days with Milky had been difficult. The lesson on Wednesday had been his worst time, but Thursday hadn't been much better.

In fact, the joy she'd first felt when she thought Milky was hers had been tarnished somewhat over the past two days. Milky didn't seem glad to see her the way Prancer always did and always had. Milky usually did what she asked, but he did it reluctantly, almost grudgingly, as though he was responding from habit but not inclination. From riding Prancer, Lisa was used to a horse that seemed to look upon every ride and every jump as a new adventure. Milky either did what he was told to do or he didn't, but he never seemed excited about it. He had bucked both times she rode him, and though the bucks weren't hard and she'd stayed on, they seemed to come out of nowhere in a most disconcerting way. Prancer was unpredictable; Milky was more so and in a totally different way. Lisa didn't know how to handle him. She had a lot to learn.

She sighed. She was still very excited about having her own horse, and of course she and Milky would get used to each other in time. She dug a carrot out of her pocket and fed it to him. Then she fastened his halter around his head and carefully began to groom him.

ON THE TRAIL, the thin November sun shined palely through the bare branches of the trees. The ground underfoot was damp but firm, and the air was warmer than it had been in several days. Stevie breathed deeply. "Ahh," she said. "This is fabulous. Not quite as fabulous as it is in midsummer, but still fabulous." She turned in the saddle to grin at Lisa, who was riding between her and Carole. "How's Milky?" She knew that Lisa had been worried before.

Lisa smiled. "He's doing pretty well," she said. "He's not acting afraid of anything. And I think he likes being out with Belle and Starlight."

"Good," Stevie said. "Our horses have to be friends, you know, just like we are."

"Of course," Lisa said. "I think Milky can hold up his end of the bargain. Give help whenever help is necessary—"

"And be totally people-crazy!" Carole said with a laugh. It was a parody of The Saddle Club rules. Carole was riding behind Lisa, so she didn't see Lisa's face fall, but Stevie did.

"What's wrong?" she asked. "Lisa? Is something wrong with Milky?"

"I don't know," Lisa confessed. She reached down to stroke Milky's neck as she talked. "So far we're not doing very well together. He hasn't done anything outrageously bad, but something about him never feels quite right to me."

"Is he lame?" Carole asked. She watched Milky's feet; they seemed to hit the ground evenly.

"No, that's not what I mean," Lisa said. "It's just—I've spent a lot of time with him over the last few days, and it's as if he doesn't care. When I ride him, he doesn't seem to like it. When I groom him, he doesn't seem to like it. It's really starting to bother me." The trail widened, and Lisa and Carole rode up so that The Saddle Club was three abreast. Stevie and Carole looked at Lisa with concern.

"Does he seem to *dislike* it when you ride him or groom him?" Carole asked.

"No. Well, sometimes," Lisa said. "It's like most of the

time he's okay with whatever I'm doing, or he's neutral about it—not pleased, maybe, but he accepts that I'm grooming him or asking him to trot in a tight circle, or whatever—and then once in a while, without warning, he seems to get upset. It's almost as if he's angry at me, but it never seems to happen for the same reason twice."

"Hmmm." Carole thought hard, but she couldn't remember any horses that had ever acted that way around her. "I'm sure he's not actually angry at you," she said. "You know horses don't have emotions the same way we do. And it's not like you're beating him up or anything."

"Of course I'm not beating him up," Lisa said. "He's my horse! But his ears go flat back against his head." In the wild, that was how horses signaled to each other that they were prepared to attack. Lisa knew it was an extreme sign.

Carole glanced at Stevie behind Lisa's head. They exchanged smiles. Both of them noticed that Lisa called Milky *her* horse. Certainly Lisa wasn't too upset over Milky's behavior.

"He feels unpredictable," Lisa continued. "He's not like Prancer at all."

Again Carole looked at Stevie, and Stevie nodded. That must be the root of Lisa's frustrations. Milky wasn't like Prancer, and Lisa loved Prancer.

"You know," Stevie said as they crossed a field where the winter grass lay in dry brown heaps, "when I first got Belle, it took me a long time to adjust to the ways she was different from Topside." Topside was the lesson horse Stevie used to ride.

38

"Really?" Lisa asked eagerly. "I never thought that about you. You always acted like making the switch was no big deal."

"That's because I was so happy to have Belle," Stevie said. "I mean, it was fantastic to have a horse of my own. Belle was pretty great, and I knew we'd learn to work things out together. Topside and I weren't supercompatible the moment we first met, either."

"I'm glad to hear you say that," Lisa said. "I kept thinking I really shouldn't be feeling so negative about Milky. I was beginning to wonder what was wrong with me."

"Nothing's wrong with you," Carole assured her friend. "Don't you remember when we first met Prancer, at the racetrack?"

"Of course," Lisa said. "I'll never forget watching her run."

"But even then her personality was out of the ordinary," Carole said. "Remember? She loved it when we groomed her and fussed over her. She loves being around people. She's excitable, but she's a very affectionate horse, especially with young riders."

"She seemed nicer than every other horse at the track," Lisa remembered. "I forgot, because now I'm so used to her."

"So if Milky's not a very affectionate horse, he probably seems a little standoffish," Carole guessed. "Think about Danny. Around Veronica, he acts like he doesn't like people at all." Danny was a superexpensive show horse that belonged to one of the worst snobs in the barn.

39

Lisa laughed. "But he likes us!" she said. "Ever since we took him to that school dance. I swear he remembers it." The Saddle Club had taken Danny to the dance to prove a point to Veronica. They'd been amazed when the horse had seemed to have fun.

"See?" Stevie pointed out. "Danny changed. If Milky isn't quite right now, he'll change, too. You can fix him."

"I know I can." Lisa patted Milky again. Her confidence felt fully restored. What had she been so upset about, anyway? A few bucks, a threatening look or two? Every horse bucked once in a while. "Thanks, guys. I'm so glad I talked to you."

"No problem," Stevie said. "That's what The Saddle Club is for."

"Did I tell you that he's actually a Thoroughbred?" Lisa asked. She felt herself getting excited about Milky all over again. Thoroughbreds had always been her favorite breed.

"Really?" Carole asked.

"Max showed me his tattoo," Lisa said. "He said he didn't know whether Milky had ever been a racehorse or not, but that probably he had been." On the track, a Thoroughbred could be easily identified by the number tattooed along the inside of its upper lip.

"That's neat," Stevie said. "What else did Max say?"

Lisa warmed to her subject as she remembered their conversation. "He's still pretty young," she said, "only eight years old, but Max said he must have had lots of early training, because he started competing in horse shows four years ago."

"Wow." Carole blinked. "That is young. That can be hard on a horse."

"Max said he's won some pretty tough classes," Lisa said proudly. "He's been all over the country, because he's been owned by a lot of people."

"That's cool," Stevie said. "You'll be some competition for Carole and me, then. I hope Max lets us go to Briarwood again."

Lisa grinned. "Me too." Briarwood was a prestigious show that Max occasionally let his students enter. Lisa had ridden Prancer there back when Prancer first came to Pine Hollow. Prancer had performed horribly; in fact, she'd been eliminated for kicking a judge. But Prancer learned, Lisa thought. She would never do that now. Lisa felt cheered by the recollection of what had been a very embarrassing day. Surely between now and the Briarwood show, she and Milky would be a team just as she and Prancer were now. With his experience and his elegance, they would set the show on its ear.

"I can't wait," she gushed. "Maybe—Aahhh!" Lisa's words turned into a yell of surprise as, without warning, Milky bucked, whirled, and tried to bolt back to the stable. Lisa fought for her balance. Milky broke into a gallop.

"Sit up!" Carole yelled. "Keep his head up!" Horses couldn't buck properly when their heads were above their shoulders.

"Hang on!" Stevie hollered as Lisa and Milky disappeared into the pine woods. She and Carole quickly turned their horses and followed, trotting so as not to incite Milky to further speed.

As soon as they reached the woods, they could see Lisa struggling with her mount. She was leaning back far enough that Milky couldn't unseat her, and she was pulling hard on the reins. Milky had slowed to a near walk. When he saw the other horses, he relaxed and allowed them to come up to him.

"Whoa." Lisa gradually let up on the reins. Milky walked forward as though he had done nothing wrong. But Lisa's heart was hammering, and her hands were shaking. "What was that about?" she asked her friends. "That's exactly what I'm talking about: One moment he's fine, and the next moment he's completely weird. Then he goes back to normal. It's eerie."

Carole and Stevie exchanged puzzled glances. "I don't know," Stevie said. "But it is his first trail ride, after all. Maybe he just suddenly decided that he was too far from home."

"Maybe," Carole said. "Or he could have been spooked by something we never even noticed. Once, I thought Starlight was getting all worked up over nothing, and it turned out there was a groundhog sitting next to the trail."

"But he just doesn't feel like he's *afraid* of something," Lisa said. "He feels like he doesn't like me."

"He doesn't know you yet, Lisa," Carole said patiently. She'd never met a horse that wasn't capable of developing a strong rapport with people. "And you don't know him. You just have to give him more time."

"He'll be wonderful," Stevie said supportively. "You can do it."

Lisa smiled. "I know I can," she said. "I'm willing to take the time with him. It's not everyone who's lucky enough to be given a nice horse like Milky." She stroked his neck tentatively. "Do you guys mind if we head back to the stables now?"

Stevie and Carole readily agreed. Lisa was glad to have two such understanding friends. She felt as if she was definitely going to need their help. Milky was going to be her horse—her dream come true—and even if he wasn't exactly the horse she would have chosen for herself, well, she was going to have to make do.

But I can fix him, Lisa said to herself. *Patience and understanding. And time. That's all any horse needs.*

CAROLE AND STEVIE peeked around the corner of the stable aisle. Halfway down, Lisa was grooming Milky on a set of cross-ties. The horse stood calmly with a bored, half-asleep expression on his face, and Lisa, brushing his tail, looked completely absorbed.

"See," Stevie whispered, "they're doing fine together."

"I know," Carole said. "I can't understand why Lisa keeps saying he doesn't like her. He seems to like her as well as he likes anyone—and he doesn't seem to be a bad horse to me." It was Sunday afternoon, and The Saddle Club had agreed to meet for another trail ride. They'd gone out on one the day before, too, and even though Milky had for the most part behaved well, Lisa hadn't wanted to go any faster than a slow trot. She hadn't wanted to jump at all. Her friends were concerned because even after four days of riding him, Lisa was still so tentative around him.

"He bucks some," Stevie admitted, "but I haven't seen him do anything really bad. All Thoroughbreds are high-strung."

"I know," Carole said. "Sometimes I wonder if a Thoroughbred is really the best kind of horse for Lisa. She's a little high-strung, too."

"A Thoroughbred is the kind of horse she's got," Stevie pointed out. "Anyway, I just wanted to see what they were like on their own, and now we know. They both seem fine."

"They'll be fine," Carole agreed. "We just need to keep encouraging her. She'll get to know Milky soon."

The girls walked down the aisle, and Lisa greeted them happily. "He's in a really good mood today," she told them. She had spent almost the entire weekend at Pine Hollow fussing over Milky and was delighted to think that she already saw improvement in him.

"Good!" Stevie patted Milky's nose. "He looks fantastic. Ready to hit the trails?"

"Just about," Lisa said. She put the comb she was using into her grooming bucket. "How's the dialogue coming, Carole?"

Carole rolled her eyes. "I can say it in my sleep. In fact, I probably have been. Listen." She recited the words.

Lisa nodded. "It sounds a lot better," she said. "You're

very smooth, and you're not pausing between the words anymore. And I think you're starting to roll your *r*s."

"Do you think so?" Carole looked delighted. "I just want to do well on this one exercise. Then I'll feel like I can do the rest."

"You'll be awesome," Stevie predicted. "How could you not be?" Stevie guessed that she had heard Carole's dialogue 356 times since Friday afternoon. She thought *she* could probably recite it in her sleep—and Lisa was definitely developing the ability to roll her own *r*s. But Stevie didn't say anything. She couldn't imagine feeling this upset about schoolwork, even given Max's academic policy. Of course Carole wasn't going to fail again! Stevie'd always been able to get decent grades in any subject once she'd put her mind to it, and she knew Carole could, too. But no matter what, she wanted Carole to be happy. "You can recite it for us a few more times on the trail," she said.

"I sound just like the tape," Carole told them proudly. She went to get her saddle.

Stevie and Lisa looked at each other and giggled.

"Do you?" Stevie asked.

"Oh, yeah," Lisa said. "I sound like the tape, too. I only know four lines of French, but I know them very well."

Stevie shook her head. "As hard as Carole's worked, she can't possibly get anything but an A."

ON THE TRAIL Milky behaved as well as he ever had, and Lisa felt her spirits soaring. Carole and Stevie were right—Milky just took a little more work than the other

46

horses Lisa had known. But he was worth it—he was hers, or he would be soon. She felt herself relaxing, and Milky seemed to respond. He mouthed the bit, and his gaits lengthened and softened.

"Want to try a canter?" Stevie suggested. She could see that Lisa and Milky were doing much better together.

"Sure!" Lisa signaled Milky, and the gelding struck out into a beautiful canter, controlled but rhythmic. "Good boy!" she praised him.

Stevie and Carole looked at each other and smiled. "You will be beating us at Briarwood," Stevie said.

Lisa laughed. "Isn't he fabulous?"

"Let's jump the log around the corner," Carole suggested. It was a little one only about a foot high, and they usually incorporated it into their trail rides. Carole glanced over at Lisa, who looked slightly uneasy but nodded. Carole brought Starlight back to a calm but steady trot, and they jumped the log in one fluid motion. Stevie and Belle followed. Carole halted Starlight and turned to watch Lisa. Lisa held the reins short as though expecting Milky to do something wrong, but Milky went over the log just as easily as Belle and Starlight had. Lisa's expression, when they landed, was one of relief.

Stevie turned Belle. "Let's do that again!"

"Let's not," Lisa said. She added quickly, "Milky did so well—I want him to end on a good jump."

"He only did one jump!" Stevie protested before catching a quelling look from Carole. She shrugged. "Sure, whatever you want," she said.

"I think I'm actually ready to go back to the barn," Lisa said. "I longed Milky this morning, you know, so he's had a lot of work today, and he's being so good I don't want to mess it up."

Stevie frowned. Milky was being good, but it wasn't as though the trail ride was difficult or anything. Most horses loved being out in the woods. Lisa was not usually this timid a rider—she was always trying new things with Prancer.

Still, Stevie thought she understood. Milky was going to be Lisa's own horse. Lisa would be responsible for everything about him, from what he was fed to how he behaved. And Lisa was the type of person who took her responsibilities very seriously. She was bound to be a little edgy about him for a while.

STEVIE AND CAROLE cared for their horses and then left for home. Lisa decided to stay. Milky's mane was long and scraggly—she'd take care of that and spend more time getting to know him.

Lisa got a step stool and a small comb and tied Milky in the aisle. The best way to trim and thin a horse's mane was to pull all the longer hairs out. Lisa had been horrified when she'd first seen this done, but she soon realized that it didn't hurt the horse. It was a time-consuming job. Lisa set her stool close to Milky's front feet, climbed onto it, and began to pull the hairs at the base of Milky's mane.

Milky relaxed his head and seemed to almost fall asleep. Lisa hummed a tune to herself. This business of having her own horse was harder than she'd expected, but it was all starting to work out. Soon, no doubt, she'd grow to love Milky.

Max came in with Red. They waved to Lisa. She waved back. She combed a thin section of Milky's mane, wrapped the long hairs around the back of the comb, and pulled. The hairs came out. Lisa dropped them to the floor and started over, moving farther up Milky's neck.

"Au Lait," she whispered to herself. It had a certain ring to it, but the problem was, so many people couldn't pronounce it. Lisa shuddered to think of herself being announced at a horse show, *"Lisa Atwood, riding Au Lait,"* and hearing it rhyme with *splat*. No matter what, Lisa thought, a horse's name shouldn't rhyme with anything awful. But she did like the idea of the name referring to the horse's color. *Maybe Blizzard*, she thought. *"Lisa Atwood, riding Blizzard."* Maybe not. It rhymed with *wizard*, which was good, but also with *gizzard*.

Snowstorm. That was a good one! Then she could call him Snowy, or even Stormy, like the book. She imagined the sign she'd have made for his stall: SNOWSTORM, OWNED BY LISA ATWOOD. She'd have it made out of wood, like the sign on Starlight's door. She paused for a moment to rest her hands.

Without warning, Milky whipped his head around, his teeth bared. Lisa jumped back, falling off her stool. The cross-tie on Milky's halter kept him from swinging his head all the way around, but even so his teeth closed on the sleeve of her jacket. He just missed her wrist.

49

"Milky!" Lisa cried. Milky rolled his eyes at her and tried to whip his head around again. His ears were flat against his skull. Lisa was so startled she felt tears come to her eyes. What was wrong with this horse?

"Lisa!" She looked up to see Max hurrying toward her. "Did that horse just try to bite you? What in the world is going on?" Max looked very upset.

"N-No," Lisa stammered. "He didn't bite me."

"But it looked like that was what he was trying to do." Max put his arm on Lisa's shoulder and pulled her back a little way from the horse. "Has he done anything like this before—ever? Anything, while you've been riding him or caring for him?"

"No," Lisa said. "He's never tried to bite." She wiped at the tear rolling down her cheek.

"You have to tell me if he ever does anything wrong," Max said. "Anything that upsets you. I want to know all about it. Remember, he's only here on trial."

Lisa swallowed hard. It sounded as if Max was ready to send Milky away! "No, Max," she made herself say in a calmer voice. "He startled me just now, but I don't really think he was trying to bite me. I think he was going after a horsefly on his neck, and I just happened to be in the way."

Max raised his eyebrows. "A horsefly in November?"

"Or something like that," Lisa said. "I'm pretty sure I saw something flying."

Max shrugged. "Well, it could be. But remember—you need to tell me if he does anything like this again."

"Sure," Lisa said. She looked at Milky. The horse had resumed standing still, half-asleep. "He seems fine now."

"Yes, he does. Let me know if you have trouble."

"Okay," Lisa promised. Max nodded to her and went back to his work.

Lisa picked up her stool and moved it closer to Milky's neck. She fingered the rip in her sleeve. None of the horses at Pine Hollow ever bit people—Lisa knew it was considered a pretty extreme vice. Horses were supposed to respect their riders, not try to hurt them.

Of course, students weren't supposed to lie to their teachers, either, the way Lisa had just lied to Max. She felt very uncomfortable about it. But the longer she thought about it, the more she was convinced that there must have been a fly or some other reasonable explanation for Milky's behavior.

Why not tell Max the truth? she asked herself. She'd never said a word about Milky bucking or trying to run back to the barn. She'd only told the other members of The Saddle Club that she felt sure Milky didn't like her.

If you tell the truth, you might lose Milky, she answered in her mind. She wasn't about to lose her dream come true. She wasn't giving him up.

Lisa sighed and gingerly started to work on Milky's mane again. She wasn't giving him up. She'd just have to make him behave better.

6

"Carole! Hey, Carole!" Lisa ran down the nearly empty hallway. It was the next day, and school was finally over. Lisa had been held up for a few minutes at the end of her last class, and she'd been a little surprised not to find Carole standing by her locker waiting for her. Now she could see that Carole was still standing by the open door of her own locker. "Hi!" Lisa said, rushing up to her friend. "How'd it go? Ready to ride?"

Carole turned her head, and Lisa was appalled to see tears filling her eyes. "What's wrong?" Lisa asked.

Carole could hardly bring herself to say it. "I failed my French dialogue again. Another F."

"Oh no! Lisa said. "But you knew it perfectly!"

Carole stood transfixed in the hallway. Tears started to

trail down her cheeks. Lisa grabbed Carole's last few notebooks and stuffed them into her backpack, then shut Carole's locker and guided her out to the street. The sooner they could get away from the school, the better.

"What happened?" Lisa asked as they made their way toward Pine Hollow.

Carole shook her head dully. "I want to quit," she said. "If I could quit a class, I would. But I can't. I have to go back there tomorrow."

"But you knew it cold," Lisa said. "Did you study the wrong dialogue?"

Carole shook her head. She swallowed hard. "No," she said. "I really did know it. At home I sounded just like the voice on the tape. But I was so nervous. I got up in front of the class and my knees were shaking, and I knew everyone could see. And I said the first word, and my voice was shaking and I didn't say it right. And then I just froze. I couldn't do anything right after that."

"Oh, Carole," Lisa moaned. "Oh, how awful."

"I was awful," Carole said. "I just kept making mistakes, and feeling worse, and making more mistakes. Even when Mr. Norris tried to help. I don't blame him for failing me again—I deserved to fail. I can't do it. I just can't speak French."

"Yes, you can," Lisa said. "You were speaking French all weekend. You were great."

"I'm not great at school," Carole said, shaking her head. "I can't do it. I just can't."

Lisa squeezed Carole's hand sympathetically. "Of

53

course you can," she assured her. "We'll help you figure it out. We'll find a way."

Carole looked down at her feet. "I just can't," she repeated. Lisa didn't know what else to say.

When they got to Pine Hollow they found Stevie waiting for them. "Bad day," Lisa said. She told Stevie what had happened to Carole, and Carole went over and put her arms around Starlight's neck.

"Oh no," Stevie moaned. Carole looked up at them.

"At least my horse doesn't have a French name like yours does, Lisa," she said bitterly. "Then I'd feel like a *total* failure."

Stevie gave Carole a hug. "Let's tack up fast," she said. "The sooner you're on a horse, the better you'll feel. And we can talk about how to help you while we're riding."

"I don't think you can help me," Carole said. "Not unless you want to come to my class and recite these things for me." She left to get her riding gear.

Stevie looked at Lisa. "Phew! She's really upset!"

"I know." Lisa was thinking about what Carole had said. What if Carole were the one riding—and owning— Milky? *Carole would probably already have all the horse's problems solved,* Lisa thought sadly. She felt like a failure, too. She hadn't yet told her friends that Milky had tried to bite her. After all, he probably hadn't really meant to bite her. There could have been a fly. Lisa looked down the aisle. Milky's beautiful face looked back at her from the door of his stall. Despite her mood, Lisa smiled. He was so beautiful—and he was hers. Or would be hers. As long as she didn't mess everything up.

"Lisa?" Stevie's voice interrupted her thoughts. "Aren't you coming?"

"Oh—right." Lisa went to get ready to ride. She had saved the carrot sticks from her lunch for Milky, and she was pleased when the horse gobbled them enthusiastically. He stood quietly while she groomed and saddled him.

"Cheer up, Carole," she heard Stevie say. "We'll figure it out."

"I just can't do it," Carole repeated.

"Yes, you can. You're not a quitter."

Neither am I, thought Lisa as she quickly tacked Milky up. She stroked his graceful neck before buckling the straps on his bridle. *I've never been a quitter, and I won't start being one now.*

Stevie and Carole weren't quite ready, so Lisa took Milky outside, checked his girth, and mounted. She walked him a few steps forward, then let him stand while she adjusted one of the stirrup leathers. Milky seemed completely calm.

Then, without warning, he threw his head down and bucked hard. Lisa scrambled to hold on. She grabbed the reins halfway up Milky's neck and hauled on his head, and Milky came to a halt. A moment later he seemed once more to be completely calm.

Lisa's heart hammered. What was wrong with this horse? How could he act so spooked and the next minute act as if nothing on earth was wrong?

"Geez, Lisa," said Stevie, coming out of the stable leading Belle, "you look like you've seen a ghost." She'd never seen Lisa's face so white.

"It's M-Milky," Lisa stammered. "He just bucked—again. He almost threw me off, and then he went back to standing like nothing was bothering him."

Stevie looked at Milky's placid, almost bored expression. She couldn't imagine that the horse had really bucked. Probably he'd just been startled by a scrap of paper or a blown leaf or something. Lots of Thoroughbreds were skittish. Stevie shook her head. She could see that whatever the horse had done had really upset Lisa.

"What's wrong?" Carole asked as she came out of the stable.

"Milky's still upsetting Lisa," Stevie said.

"He scared me," Lisa admitted. She described the way Milky had bucked. For some reason, she held off telling her friends about the bite. *Probably it didn't really happen like that,* she thought. "I can't tell if he's really bad or if I'm making him out to be worse than he is," she admitted to her friends.

Stevie nodded. "I haven't seen him do anything too horrible," she said, "but I can see that he's making you nervous."

"We'll talk about it while we ride," Carole said. She mounted and stood in her stirrups to flex her legs. "Are you okay to go out on the trails?"

"I guess so," Lisa said. "As long as we go slowly." Carole looked over at Stevie. Stevie shrugged and shook her head. Milky was doing nothing whatsoever for Lisa's confidence.

"YOU KNOW," STEVIE said once they were out of sight of the barn and had reached a place where they could ride three abreast, "I think there are a lot of similarities between your problem, Carole, and Lisa's."

Carole frowned. "I was pretty much kidding when I said I was glad my horse didn't have a French name," she said. "I mean, I am glad, but I don't see that Lisa's horse has anything to do with my problem."

"No, listen," Stevie persisted. "I didn't say they were the same, I said they were similar. Originally, you had a lot of trouble pronouncing the French, right?" Carole nodded. "But you worked hard on it, and before class today you knew it—I know you did, Carole. I heard you say it forty times, and I heard the tape, too. You were good. But in class today you couldn't recite it well because you got too nervous."

Carole nodded. "True, but how does that—"

Stevie held up her hand. "And look at the way Lisa's riding. She's clearly worried about what Milky's going to do next."

Lisa looked down. It was true that she was riding with her reins shorter than usual and with her heels more forward and her shoulders farther back—defensive riding, Max called it. "You would be, too," Lisa said. "He keeps bucking."

"I know," Stevie said soothingly. "But it might be that part of the reason he's bucking is because he can tell that you're nervous. He's a Thoroughbred, and you know how sensitive they are to their riders' emotional states. It's like with Carole. Your nervousness wasn't the start of your problem—he was already misbehaving the first day you rode him—but now it's making your problem worse. He dumped Jessica that first day, so when you got on him you were already expecting him to misbehave. But back then he was probably just acting up because he was in a strange environment. Only now, whenever you ride him, you're nervous, and he acts up, and that makes you more nervous, and that makes him more likely to act up."

Lisa felt a flush of relief. What Stevie was suggesting made sense. Maybe Milky's problems really were all her fault by now. That would be best. She could fix what she was doing wrong, and Milky would turn out fine.

"Okay," Carole said. "I think you're right, about me at least, and maybe about Lisa, too. I did know that dialogue before I got up to recite it. But how on earth are Lisa and I supposed to keep from being nervous? Believe me, if I could have stopped my knees or voice from shaking this afternoon, I would have done it."

Stevie shook her head. "I have absolutely no idea."

58

Carole had to laugh. "Lisa, you're the actress. You've dealt with stage fright. Any suggestions?"

Lisa had been in a few community plays. She thought for a moment. "I'll tell you the truth," she said. "When I'm up onstage, the stage lights are so bright I can hardly see the audience. I just don't even think of them very much. And then, I've rehearsed my part so many times that I automatically know what to say and do." She looked down at the horse she was riding. "With Milky I don't get a rehearsal. I never know what my part is."

"Maybe that would help Carole, though," Stevie said.

"What? Stage lights?"

"No, rehearsals. When you practice your dialogue, how do you do it?

"I just say it," Carole said. "You've heard me."

"So, maybe you should pretend you're doing it in front of your class," suggested Stevie. "Make yourself stand in front of an empty room and recite, and imagine that the room is full of your classmates."

Carole wrinkled her nose. "I guess that might help. At this point I'll admit that I'm willing to try almost anything." She sighed. "I wish I was the one with the horse problem. This is all so different from horses. Whenever I've had a major problem in the past, I've been able to connect it with horses somehow, and it always helped me."

They walked on for a few minutes. The only sounds were the clinking of the horses' bits and the thunk when a hoof hit a stone.

"Here we go," Stevie said at last. "I've got it. Horse shows."

"French class is like horse shows?" Carole was puzzled.

"Yes!" Stevie sounded triumphant. "Before a horse can do well in a show, he has to feel comfortable. Before he can feel comfortable, he has to get used to the show routine."

"Well, sure," Carole said. "That's why Max likes to take his young horses to shows and not enter them in any classes."

"That's right," Lisa said. "He puts them in the trailer, and at the show he leaves them in a stall for a while, and then he walks or rides them all around the grounds, so they can see everything that's going on." She snorted. "If I'd done that with Prancer before our first show, it might have helped."

"Like a dress rehearsal," Stevie said. "Remember, horses have to be taught everything in small steps. They don't ever understand a complicated situation right away."

Carole grinned. For the first time, she actually felt better. "I guess French is the most complicated situation I've faced this year. Maybe I can break my training down into little steps—my training for being in the classroom as well as for actually saying the dialogue. I can learn one step at a time. And maybe if I think about it in terms of little steps instead of as one great big problem, I won't get so nervous in the first place. Thanks, Stevie."

"Don't thank me," Stevie said. "Thank Max. He's the one who taught us this."

"But you're the one who connected it to French and to Milky."

"Do you think trying to work in little steps will help with Milky, Lisa?" Stevie asked.

"Oh, yes!" Lisa said. She felt relieved, and also rather sorry for Milky. "I never thought of how confusing he must find a new stable like Pine Hollow. And then to have a scared-stiff rider on his back! No wonder he's been acting so strange! I'll have to go more slowly with him."

Carole shook her head. "I don't think you should take too much of the blame for this yourself," she said. "You are riding him defensively, but you haven't turned into a block of wood. It's not as if you're acting scared stiff. And you have been taking things slowly with him. Max would say so, too."

"But obviously not slowly enough," Lisa said.

Carole wasn't sure she agreed. What Stevie suggested made sense, but on the other hand, why would Lisa describe herself as scared stiff? Why would she think Milky was that bad? "Maybe Milky's more sensitive than most horses," she said.

"I think he is," Lisa said.

Carole nodded. Once again it crossed her mind that Lisa, of all people, did not need an extremely sensitive horse. But then, Max must have helped choose Milky for Lisa. Max must know what he was doing.

Lisa saw the doubt in Carole's face and thought she knew what her friend was thinking. Lisa agreed: Milky probably wasn't the type of horse she'd most like to have. But she wondered if she had a choice. Something had prompted her parents and Max to select this horse for her. If she turned it down, they might think she still didn't want a horse. Milky, Lisa feared, was her only option.

"SMALL STEPS," CAROLE said to Lisa as they mounted their horses in preparation for their usual Tuesday lesson.

Lisa smiled. "Small steps," she agreed. She would be firm with Milky, but she wouldn't expect too much from him. And, no matter what, she would not let herself get too nervous. "Speaking of that," she said to Carole, "how's French?"

Carole made a face. "It's coming, I guess. I made myself stand up at the front of our living room last night and recite our next dialogue to my father. That did make me feel more nervous than just reciting to you and Stevie, so I guess it's an improvement of sorts. I have to do this new one in class tomorrow."

Lisa nodded. "Good luck."

"To you, too," Carole said. She made a motion toward Milky. Lisa looked down at the horse and took a deep breath. *Small steps,* she reminded herself. She walked Milky out to the rail and started trotting to warm him up before the class began.

"ALL RIGHT, HERE'S your course," Max said. It was midway through the lesson, and the riders were ready to start jumping fences. "The brush box to the pair of white verticals—four strides in between them—to the blue gate, then around the corner to the rolltop. Got that? Lisa, start us off."

The other riders moved their horses to the rail, where they would be out of Lisa's way. Lisa traced her finger in the air to fix the course in her mind, then nodded at Max and sent Milky toward the brush box. She reminded herself to breathe normally. Milky—and Max—mustn't be able to tell how nervous she was.

The brush box came up more quickly than Lisa expected. Milky jumped big, and Lisa had to throw her hands forward to keep from hitting him in the mouth. She bit her lip in concentration and looked for her next fence.

"Straight into the corner," Max coached her. "Then turn, turn, use your left leg. Get straight to the jump—" Milky plunged over the first white fence, took four canter strides, and jumped the second. A bit short, Lisa thought, but better than the week before. She steadied him around the corner and, her confidence increasing, sent him toward the gate.

Milky stopped in front of it. Lisa felt her shoulders and hands drop as he put on the brakes. Her confidence dropped as well.

"That's okay," Max said encouragingly. "Give him some leg, and ride like you really want him to jump."

I want him to jump, Lisa thought, *but what I* really *want is not to fall off him when he stops.* She didn't say anything to Max. She picked up a trot, circled Milky, and came at the fence again, concentrating very hard. Milky slowed but then jumped. "Good boy!" Lisa said.

"Good! Now the rolltop," said Max.

Lisa sat up and drove Milky through the turn. The rolltop was an odd-looking fence made of solid wood. *That will really hurt if I land on it*, Lisa thought. She shook her head, squared her shoulders, and kept going. She would not let herself be afraid—or at any rate, she would not let her fear keep her from riding.

"Steady," Max said. "He doesn't need that much leg. You're pushing him too hard, Lisa—" But Milky jumped the rolltop anyway, and Lisa let out a gasp of relief. The course was over.

"Good job," Max said. "How did that feel?"

"Fine," Lisa answered.

"You're looking upset. Is he bothering you?"

"No, not at all." Lisa patted Milky's neck. She trotted him past the line of waiting riders to take her place at the end, and Polly started her horse, Romeo, on course. As Lisa rode past Carole, Milky kicked out at Starlight, suddenly and viciously. He missed, but Starlight squealed. Lisa pushed Milky forward, and Carole got Starlight out of the way.

"If he kicks, keep him away from the other horses," Max told Lisa. "Has he kicked before?" Lisa shook her head. She halted Milky a little distance behind the others. Carole and Stevie turned to look at her.

"Is Starlight okay?" Lisa asked.

Carole nodded. "He's fine. How about you?"

"I'm fine." Lisa felt a surge of irritation. Why was everyone asking her how she felt? Did they think she wasn't a good enough rider to have a horse of her own? "Just wait," she whispered to Milky. "When we're at Briarwood . . ." But it was now even harder to imagine competing Milky at Briarwood than it had been the week before. *Small steps*, Lisa reminded herself. She and Milky would be ready for Briarwood in plenty of time to compete.

Stevie turned to Carole. "Is Starlight really okay?" she whispered, being careful to keep her voice low. Max hated it when his students talked during lessons.

"Yes. Milky didn't make contact," Carole whispered back. "He just tried to. What do you think about Lisa? She's riding with so much control today, but it looks like she's having to work awfully hard to keep that control."

"I don't know," Stevie said. "So far she and Milky are doing a lot better than they were last week."

66

"Except that Lisa looks a lot less happy."

"Milky's not acting worse than Prancer on one of her bad days," said Stevie. "And Lisa's coping just fine. She rode to that rolltop really well."

"I know," Carole said. "I just wish she was having more fun."

"She'll have plenty of fun when she gets to know Milky a little better," Stevie said. Carole nodded. What Stevie said was probably true.

"Stevie Lake, do you plan on riding with us today?" Max asked in a tone of voice that said he knew she'd been talking.

"Sorry." Stevie sent Belle forward. She made a mental note to ask Lisa about Milky after class.

As it happened, Stevie didn't have to, because Max beat her to it. Before Lisa had a chance to dismount, Max walked over and stood by Milky's shoulder. "Are you getting along with him okay?" he asked her.

Lisa didn't know how to respond. Milky had refused to jump a few more times during the lesson, but he hadn't kicked out again, and Lisa felt she had done a good job of keeping him under control. On the other hand, she was worn out from the effort she'd expended, and she still didn't feel comfortable on his back. Something about his personality kept her on edge. But she could hardly say that to Max, who might decide to take Milky away from her.

"I think we're doing pretty well," she said at last. "He's calmer than he was last week. I'm trying to go slowly with him, you know, to give him a chance to get used to everything."

Max nodded, but he didn't look convinced. "Are you sure you feel okay on him?" he asked. "You're a lot more tense with him than you are with Prancer."

"I just need to get used to him, Max," Lisa protested. "I'm riding him a lot. We just need more time."

"I've noticed the amount of time you've put in with him," Max replied. "I appreciate it, but don't feel like it's something you have to do."

Lisa bit her lip. Of course she had to spend this much time with Milky! How else was she going to solve his problems? "But I want to," she protested. "Carole and Stevie helped me work out a training plan for him. Tomorrow I'm going to work him in the back field." Carole and Stevie both had after-school appointments that would keep them away from the stable, and Lisa didn't want to take Milky on a trail ride alone. The back field was a nice compromise.

"Don't you have piano lessons on Wednesdays?" Max said.

"Oh, I'm skipping it this week," Lisa said. "I skip lots of times. I'd rather work with Milky." She looked at Stevie and Carole, who were waiting for her to finish. "It'll be fun," she told them. "More fun than piano, anyway."

"You don't need to do that," Max said.

"But I want to!" Lisa said. She dismounted and gave Milky a hearty pat on the shoulder. "I'm having lots of fun with him! Really. I am."

"I know I suggested that you ride another horse," Max continued, "but it doesn't have to be Milky. You can ride Topside, if you want. Or Barq, or almost any of them."

"Max! I'd rather ride Milky." Lisa thought longingly of Topside's gentle manner. There was nothing scary about Topside at all. *The difference,* Lisa thought, *is that my parents don't want to buy me Topside.*

"Okay, then." Max seemed to relent. "But if you have any trouble with him, I want you to let me know. I was surprised, after how well you said he was doing, to see him still having this many problems in our lesson today."

Max walked back to the office. Carole and Stevie looked at Lisa. Lisa looked at the ground.

"Haven't you been telling Max about the trouble you've been having?" Carole asked curiously. "He might have some good ideas about how to help."

"Or he might just decide that I'm not a good enough rider for Milky," Lisa said. "And when he says that to my mother, she might decide that I don't need my own horse after all. Besides, Milky hasn't actually been that bad. I mean, I've never even fallen off him, and I've fallen off Prancer plenty of times."

Carole nodded. She could understand how Lisa felt. If she'd been in Lisa's position, she wouldn't have wanted to do anything to jeopardize her chances of getting a horse, either. Carole looked at Starlight's soft, expressive face. Not for the first time, she thought how lucky she was to own a horse like him.

* * *

69

THAT NIGHT STEVIE called Carole to talk privately before getting Lisa on the line. "I'm kind of worried about her," Stevie confessed. "When Max said she didn't look like she was having any fun—after you said she didn't look like she was having any fun—I realized that Lisa hasn't looked like she's been having fun all week. I think she's really letting this stuff with Milky get her down."

Carole agreed. "Lisa's such a perfectionist. She wants Milky to be super right away, and he's just not going to be."

"And I think Lisa's worried about her riding ability, too," Stevie said. "You know how she is. Getting As in all her classes. It's hard for her whenever things don't come easily."

"I know," Carole said. "I'm not sure what to do for her. I'll be happy to help her with Milky's training plan, but I don't think his training is really the problem. After all, he's won ribbons at top horse shows. He should know what he's doing."

"I think the problem is Lisa's confidence," Stevie said. "I think we need to remind her how well she's doing." Carole agreed. "I'll just call her up now," Stevie said, punching the numbers on the phone.

AT HOME LISA sat at her desk, working on her math homework. There was something comforting about math. With math, you either had the right answer or you didn't. There were no nuances, no tricky pronunciations, no degrees of right or wrong. Not like with Milky, who was neither exactly wrong nor exactly right, but somewhere in between. Lisa sighed and put down her pencil. She rubbed her forehead. Somehow she had to figure out what to do about Milky.

That afternoon she had overheard another fragment of a conversation between her mother and Max. Actually, "overheard" was stretching the truth. Ever since she'd heard her mother talking to Max the week before, Lisa had kept her ears open for a second opportunity. When she heard her mother say, "Oh, Max! Why not?" she'd gotten up from the living room couch, walked into the dining room, and listened through the door.

"Well," her mother had said with a touch of exasperation, "not ready is not ready, I suppose. But I do hope it won't take much longer. Okay, I'll call back next week."

Lisa had been holding her breath. So, despite all the assurances she'd given him, Max still didn't think she was ready to have Milky for her own! Lisa was annoyed, but a secret part of her also felt relieved. Then she felt annoyed at feeling relieved. Now she mostly felt sad. Wasn't getting a horse supposed to be one of the most exciting things that could happen to her? It had been for Carole and Stevie.

The phone rang. It was her friends, and they both sounded so cheerful that they made her head hurt worse.

"I'm doing my math homework and trying to pretend I'm not worried about Milky," she told them. Suddenly Lisa wanted to unburden herself and tell her friends everything. "It's not been going well. Last week—"

"That's why we wanted to call you," Stevie broke in. "We thought you looked unhappy today, and all last week. We're worried that you might be letting yourself get too upset about Milky."

"It depends on how you define *too upset*," Lisa said. "Sometimes I think I'm not letting myself get upset enough."

"But you're really doing well with him," Stevie said soothingly. "Today's lesson was much better than last week's. We don't want you to feel bad. You're making great progress, you're a great rider, and we know you can do this."

"That's right," Carole said. "I know how easy it is to feel down when you want to do something better than you are—that's exactly where I am with my French class. But you are doing a good job with him, Lisa. Some horses are just more difficult than others."

"You really think so?" Lisa asked. "I haven't been feeling like I was doing a good job."

"See?" Stevie said. "That's why we wanted to cheer you up. You're not giving yourself enough credit. And the more discouraged you get, the harder this is going to be."

"Sometimes I'm just not sure I can fix him," Lisa said. *I'm not sure I want to,* she nearly added.

"Of course you can!" Stevie said. "We'll help you, and so will Max. You know the three of us together can do anything. Right, Carole?"

"Right," Carole said firmly. "Just think how wonderful it will be when we all three have our own horses. Now

I've got to go. Dad said he'd listen to my dialogue again, and he's invited some of the neighbors over to hear it, too. If I don't get nervous in front of Mr. and Mrs. Grundy, I'm not going to get nervous anywhere. They're flakes."

Lisa laughed. "Good night. And thanks, guys."

"Any time," Stevie said cheerfully. "Help whenever help is needed—The Saddle Club way."

The problem, Lisa thought after she hung up the phone, was that even if Stevie and Carole helped her with Milky, in the end he was going to be her horse, not theirs. She was the one who was going to have to cope with him every day, not them.

Well then, I'll just have to cope with him, Lisa thought. *I'm not giving up this chance. Next week Max will have to tell Mom that I'm ready for Milky, because I will be.* She sharpened her pencil and went back to her math.

"LISA!" CAROLE GRABBED her friend by the arms and twirled her around in the school hallway. "I did it! I passed my French dialogue!"

"Fantastic!" Lisa beamed at her. "I knew you could."

Carole rolled her eyes. "It still wasn't perfect— a C-plus. But the great part is, I started to mess up again."

"That was the great part? Why?"

Carole laughed. "I started to mess up," she explained, "but then I got myself back under control. I made it through the rest without any big mistakes."

"Oh," Lisa said, understanding. "That's really cool. Now maybe you won't feel so nervous next time."

"I'll be so nervous I could die," Carole predicted, still

laughing. "But it won't matter. I passed this time, and I can pass again."

"And you'll be able to ride at Pine Hollow forever and ever," Lisa said.

Carole nodded. "Except for today. But if this school meeting gets out on time, I'll be there later. I probably won't have time to ride, though."

Lisa made a face. "And Stevie's going to her orthodontist. It'll just be me and Milky."

Carole gave her a hug. "You can do it. Have fun."

" 'YOU CAN DO it,' " Lisa muttered to herself. " 'Have fun.' " She looked at Milky, who was standing calmly on the cross-ties. He was muddy from having been turned out during the day, and she had a long grooming job ahead of her. "Fun, right, Milky? You just love to be groomed?" She picked up the rubber curry. Milky laid his ears back. Lisa hesitated, but she had to be able to clean the dirt off him. She started currying his hindquarters, well out of reach of his teeth.

Well, of course I'll have fun, she told herself while she continued to work over him. *Riding is fun. The most fun thing in the world. And the absolute best part of riding is forming a partnership with your horse, and the best way to do that is to have your own horse. So here I am, enjoying the absolute best part of riding.* She grabbed a soft brush and gingerly stroked Milky's face. He put his nose in the air. *Oh, well,* Lisa thought, *his face isn't that dirty.* She put the brush back into her box.

The stables were quiet. Max had only a few students taking private lessons that day. Lisa wished that Carole and Stevie could be there. Their presence would give her confidence, just the way their conversation had the night before.

But Carole had worked through her French problem, and surely Lisa could work through her difficulties with Milky. Maybe today would be her breakthrough. And at any rate, she was going to take small steps. Today, all she wanted Milky to do was walk and trot calmly around the back field.

She finished grooming, tacked Milky up, and tightened his girth. She fastened her riding helmet and pulled on her gloves. *Better tell Max where I'm going,* she thought. She opened the door of the office. Max was talking on the phone, but he asked her what she needed and nodded when she told him where she'd be.

See, she told herself, *Max thinks I'm perfectly capable of riding Milky all by myself. That must mean I am.* But she still felt nervous. She told herself that Milky would pick up on her nerves. She had to calm down in order to be effective with him. She reminded herself to breathe.

Milky didn't stir while she lowered the stirrups and checked the girth one last time. *See,* Lisa told herself, *you're imagining things. You're making this into too big of a deal.* But after she mounted she was very careful to touch Pine Hollow's good-luck horseshoe. No one who touched it before riding had ever been seriously injured. For the first time, Lisa felt as if she might need the horseshoe's protection.

She walked Milky out to the field and carefully shut the gate behind them. It was a long enclosed meadow, larger than any of the riding rings but not as big as the giant paddock where the horses were sometimes turned loose to play. In good weather Max put fences in the field, but now only a few immovable ones dotted the brown grass. There was nothing there that Milky should find upsetting.

Lisa started Milky on a circuit of the field. She kept him at a slow walk, and he ambled along as though there was nothing interesting about what they were doing. Lisa could feel how tense her legs were against his sides. She realized that she was clenching her fingers around the reins. She shook her hands and shoulders loose and willed herself to relax.

They went once around the field, and then Lisa asked Milky to trot. He picked up the gait without fuss and moved at a fairly slow pace, not taking off with her or fighting the bit. Still, Lisa felt as though disaster was imminent. Any moment now, Milky could do something awful.

Lisa wondered why she was feeling so scared. Even when Prancer was acting her absolute worst, Lisa never felt like that. *I just don't think Milky likes me*, she thought, and then, *I don't trust him at all*. When Prancer did something strange, it always seemed as if the cause was excess energy or Thoroughbred nervousness, but Milky felt completely different. *I don't think he likes me, and I don't like him, either.*

That thought startled her. What would she do with a horse she didn't even like? What could she do?

They came to the far corner of the field. Milky dragged his hindquarters a bit through the turn, and Lisa used her inside rein to get him straight.

Without warning, Milky exploded. He leaped into the air and landed bucking. Lisa dug in with her heels and fought to stay on him. She pulled the reins in. Milky came to a standstill. "Walk," Lisa said. Her mouth was dry. She was terrified. She squeezed him forward anyway. "Walk," she said.

Milky squealed, whirled, and bucked again. Lisa fell against his neck but grabbed a big handful of mane and managed to stay on his back. One of her feet came out of its stirrup.

Milky reared up on his hind legs. Lisa screamed. Max had told them once that rearing was the most dangerous thing a horse could do, because the horse couldn't balance on two legs. It could fall over backward, crushing its rider.

Lisa clung to the saddle as Milky reared higher, reaching skyward with his front hooves. "If you're ever on a rearing horse," Max had told them, *"get off."*

At the time Lisa hadn't quite understood what he meant, but now, as Milky touched his forefeet to the ground and immediately reared again, she understood

78

that it was dangerous to be on him for even another second. She let go of the reins and Milky's mane and threw herself off to the side.

The hard ground hurt as she crashed onto her shoulder. She rolled to the side. When Milky came down, she didn't want to be within reach of his hooves. But Milky didn't seem interested in her now that she was off his back. He landed, bucked once, and ran to the other side of the field. He put his head down and began to graze.

Lisa lay on the cold, dead grass. She couldn't believe that Milky was just standing there, eating, as though he hadn't just thrown the worst fit she'd ever seen a horse throw. She couldn't believe it. Her shoulder ached where she had landed on it, but she knew it would only be bruised. Her spirit, however, was crushed. She had been scared before, but now she was petrified. Milky could have killed her. Accidents could always happen around horses, but this wouldn't have been an accident, because Milky had done it on purpose. Lisa had no doubt of that.

Lisa's shoulders started to shake. She pressed her face into the ground and let herself cry loud, heart-wrenching sobs. She didn't want this horse. She was afraid of him. She would almost rather not have a horse than have this one.

Almost. Lisa quit crying. She drew herself up into a sitting position and watched Milky graze. Part of her—most of her—wanted to give up. But if she could fix him, wouldn't he be worth it? And wouldn't she feel terrific, knowing that she'd tamed and befriended such a wild horse?

But *could* she fix him? She wiped the last traces of tears from her face and got to her feet. She just didn't know.

9

LISA WALKED SLOWLY toward Milky. He lifted his head and watched her approach, but he didn't show any signs of anger or fear. His reins hung loose under his chin, and his bit was smeared with half-chewed grass. "Steady," Lisa said, as much to herself as to Milky. She reached for the reins. Milky dropped his head to grab another bite of grass, but Lisa tugged on the reins and he gave up.

"What am I going to do with you?" she asked him. Horses didn't understand English, she knew. But she had the feeling that even if Milky could speak to her, she wouldn't trust his answer.

Still, maybe there was some logical, easily solved reason for his crazy behavior. Maybe Milky was in pain. Maybe something started hurting him when Lisa rode. Maybe there was a burr on his saddle pad.

That was it! That really could be it! It would be unusual, but it could happen. Lisa walked Milky over to the fence line and quickly stripped his saddle off. She hung it on the fence and went over the fleece saddle pad as carefully as possible, squishing the white padding between her fingers. A short piece of hay could be as sharp as a needle.

The saddle pad was clean except for a few of Milky's silver hairs. In fact, it looked as if it had been freshly washed. Lisa put it down and began to examine the saddle—maybe part of it was broken or something was stuck to it—and then the girth, but to her disappointment both seemed entirely normal.

Next she turned her attention to Milky himself. Could he have a sore or a bruise where the saddle fastened tight around him? She ran her hands over him, first lightly, then pressing hard, and watched his face and ears carefully for any change in expression. Milky looked bored, even uneasy, but he never looked as if he was feeling any sort of pain, and Lisa couldn't find any bumps or marks on his smooth skin. In the end, she had to conclude that nothing had caused him any sudden pain.

Could he be hurting from an old injury? Lisa considered the idea but discarded it. Max always had Judy Barker, Pine Hollow's veterinarian, examine any new horse before he brought it to the stable. Judy would have found any long-standing problems.

Lisa sighed. She'd been so hopeful that she would discover a logical explanation for Milky's fits. She carefully put his saddle back on. As she tightened the girth, Milky turned his head toward her and laid his ears back. "Stop it," Lisa said. She flicked the end of the reins at him. "Behave."

But when she went to put her foot into the stirrup, she found that she couldn't do it. She absolutely could not bring herself to get back on the horse.

You have to, she told herself. It was one of Max's rules: Always get back on. Every ride was supposed to end on a positive note. If Milky got to go back to his stall now, he might see it as a reward for rearing. At the very least, he wouldn't have any chance to learn that rearing was wrong. Lisa knew she had to get back on him and make him behave. Walk and trot calmly around the field, that was all.

She reached for the stirrup but again let her foot fall back to the ground. She looked around the field as though the answer to her problems could be found in some grassy corner. *How hard can this be?* she asked herself. She knew the answer: Too hard. She just couldn't make herself ride this horse.

Well, The Saddle Club could help her figure things out. She'd talk the situation over with Stevie and Carole and come up with a new plan for tomorrow. Meanwhile, she'd had enough of Milky for the day. She ran the stirrups up on the saddle and led Milky out of the field.

She was almost to the stable when Max ran out to meet

her, a worried look on his face. "What happened?" he asked. "Why are you walking him? Did you fall off?"

Lisa didn't know how to explain. "No," she said at last. "I didn't fall off." Which was not a lie, she told herself firmly. She had thrown herself off Milky on purpose.

"You're not hurt?" Max asked.

"No," Lisa said, relieved that she could answer that question entirely honestly. "I'm fine." She started walking again. Max walked beside her. He seemed to be waiting for an explanation. Lisa didn't want to give him one.

"Is the horse hurt?"

"No, Max. He's fine, too."

"Did he lose a shoe?"

"Max!" Lisa stopped. "I'm just not feeling very well today. I must be getting a cold. I started coughing when I was riding, and I just couldn't stop, so I got off. I think I'm going to go home."

Max smiled. "Well, that's good. I hope you're feeling better soon, but I'm glad you didn't have any kind of problem with the horse." He patted Milky. "I was worried there when I saw you coming back on foot."

Lisa forced herself to smile. How could she tell Max she was afraid of Milky? It was so embarrassing! She just couldn't do it. Not yet, anyway.

"Do you feel well enough to untack him before you go home?" Max asked her kindly.

"Sure," Lisa said. She coughed a little into her hand.

84

"You can use the office phone, if you need to call your mom to pick you up."

"Thanks." Lisa nodded to Max and turned Milky to lead him through the side door. She put him into his stall, took off his saddle and bridle, and shut the door on him with a feeling of total relief.

How could she be so afraid of a horse? After all, what had he really done? She thought back to the terrifying moment when he had leaped into the air, when she had clung to his mane hoping desperately that he would land on his feet. But he *hadn't* flipped. She really wasn't hurt. She hadn't been lying to Max about *that*.

Only about all the rest. She felt miserable and ashamed. Why couldn't her dream horse be like Belle or Starlight? Or Prancer or Topside or Derby or Barq? Or even little shaggy Nickel? All the Pine Hollow horses and ponies were friendly and reliable. Why did she have to get a horse like Milky?

And why couldn't she make things work out with him? If only she were a better rider, she'd probably be fine.

Lisa hung Milky's saddle and bridle in the tack room. She felt in her pockets for the carrots she had intended to give him. She'd give them to Prancer instead—to a horse she actually liked.

Prancer whinnied when she saw Lisa, and Lisa felt another wave of misery engulf her. That was what she always wanted—a horse of her own that was eager to see her. She went into Prancer's stall and gave her the carrots, then put her arms around the horse's neck and buried her face in her mane. "Oh, Prancer," she whispered, "why can't I have you?"

The truth hit Lisa full force. She did not want Milky. Not now, not ever. Not even if it meant that she wouldn't get a horse of her own.

Lisa began to cry. How could she tell her parents? And what would she say to Max?

LISA FELT HER hot tears trickle down her nose into Prancer's coat. Prancer, empathetic as always, leaned her weight against Lisa's shoulder. Lisa's tears fell faster.

"Hey!" To her surprise, Lisa heard Stevie's voice. "Lisa! We thought you'd be riding by now!"

Lisa looked up. There was Stevie—and Carole! "I'm so glad to see you," she said.

"So are we!" Stevie swung Prancer's door open and stepped inside. Carole followed. "Carole's meeting and my appointment both ended early. We were hoping we'd still have a chance to ride with you, but we thought you'd already be gone. Why aren't you with Milky?"

"I've been out and back again," Lisa said shortly. "And I'm not riding Milky anymore. Not ever again."

Stevie was more startled by Lisa's tone than by her words. "You've been crying!" she said, realizing it for the first time. "Oh no! Lisa, what's wrong?"

Lisa burst into fresh tears. "I just can't do it," she sobbed. "I can't ride that horse anymore."

"No, of course not," soothed Stevie, even though she had no idea what Lisa meant. "Here, sit down." She kicked some of the loose hay on the floor of Prancer's stall into a pile and pushed Lisa onto it. Carole closed Prancer's door and sat down facing them. Prancer watched them curiously.

"What's wrong?" Carole asked. She too was surprised to see Lisa this upset. She'd known Lisa was having trouble with Milky, but this looked like disaster.

"The worst thing happened today." In a halting voice, Lisa described how Milky had reared. "He's always like that," she said. "He does things out of nowhere, and then he acts like there's nothing wrong. He's like a bully who's out to get people. Maybe it's just me, or maybe he really hates to be ridden, but I don't care what it is. I'm just not riding him anymore. If Max gave him to me for free, I'd say no."

"Whoa," Stevie said. "We never realized you felt this bad. Right, Carole?"

"Right," Carole confirmed. "What else has he been doing?"

For the first time, Lisa told her friends how Milky had tried to bite her. She told them how he bucked whenever she rode him. "I'm afraid of him," she said. "I realized that today. I went to get back on him, and I just couldn't do it." She started crying harder. "I feel like such a failure. I really tried to make him work out."

"You're not a failure," Carole said instantly. "You're a good rider."

"If I were a better rider, I could have fixed him. If I were a better rider, I could have my own horse."

"Hogwash," Stevie said. She fished around in her pocket and found an old tissue. It had a partially eaten lollipop stuck to one end. She tore that part off and handed the rest of the tissue to Lisa, who wiped her eyes. Stevie offered the lollipop to Prancer. The mare sniffed it and turned her head away.

"Don't give her that," Lisa protested. "It's nasty."

Stevie put it back in her pocket. "She's too smart to take it, anyway. But you know, Lisa, what you just said is wrong. In the first place, we still don't know for sure that Max and your parents mean for Milky to be your horse."

"I know," Lisa said, "but it really looks as if they do."

"Right, but anyway, whether or not you get a horse probably doesn't have anything to do with how good a rider you are. And in the second place, I think you're wrong to say if you were a better rider you could fix him."

"Why?" asked Lisa. "It's true."

"Probably it isn't," Stevie said. "I didn't realize Milky was so bad before, but he sounds like a horse that's out of control, even dangerous. It's not your job to fix dangerous horses."

"Does he seem to react to anything specific that you

do?" Carole asked. "Like, does he always buck when you ask for a left-lead canter, or something like that?"

"No," Lisa said, shaking her head. "I can never connect his behavior to anything else. That's part of the reason it's so scary." She blew her nose. "Got any more tissues, Stevie?"

Carole fished through her own pockets, which were cleaner than Stevie's. "Here's one. So, if you can't connect Milky's misbehavior to anything you're doing, what makes you think you're causing it?"

"I didn't say I was causing it," Lisa argued. "I just said that if I were a better rider, I would be able to fix it." She sniffed. "If I were you, or Stevie. If I really deserved a horse of my own."

"Oh, give me a break," Stevie said. "As though whether or not you have your own horse has anything to do with whether or not you deserve one. Do you think for one minute that Veronica diAngelo deserves to have her own horse?"

Lisa thought about the rich, spoiled girl who never seemed to do anything for her beautiful horse. "No," she admitted.

"And I bet there are thousands of kids in places like . . . oh, Bangladesh, who really deserve horses but don't get them."

Lisa had to laugh. "Bangladesh!"

"Or New York City. There aren't a whole lot of horses there. Anyway, my point is, I think you're an excellent rider, and I think you deserve your own horse, but I don't think those things have anything to do with one another."

"Okay," Lisa said. "Thanks. I understand your point even if I'm not sure I agree with you. But I need to know what you guys really think about Milky. Am I just being a ninny? Should I have gotten back on him in the field?"

"No. Absolutely not," Carole said firmly. She picked up a piece of hay and twirled it between her fingertips. "I agree with Stevie that he sounds dangerous. If he's been acting the way you say he has, then you should have quit riding him days ago. When Max says always get back on, he means in a usual situation, like when you fall off and it's totally your fault, and he doesn't want you becoming afraid of riding. He doesn't mean when the horse is trying to hurt you."

"Plus," cut in Stevie, "riding is supposed to be fun. It's not supposed to be terrifying."

"Sometimes it's a little scary," Lisa said, thinking of some of her earlier experiences.

"For minutes at a time," agreed Stevie. "Not for whole days at a time."

"It's supposed to be fun even when it is a little scary," added Carole. "The fun is always supposed to be there."

Lisa sighed. "Well, I sure haven't had a lot of fun this week," she said. "I just hated to admit how awful I felt. I still feel awful. I mean—Remember, Stevie, how you said Carole's French class was like Milky? And Carole worked so hard and she got so much better?"

Carole shook her head. "They aren't the same," she said. "French is just French. I mean, it's all there, it stays the same. I just have to learn it. Everything that can change is on my side. But you and Milky are both variable—"

"You're making them sound like a math class," Stevie joked.

Carole rolled her eyes. "I mean, Lisa can change all she wants. She can be the best rider in the world, but Milky's not just an object, like a car that anyone could learn to drive. He's got his own mind. So no matter what, Lisa might not be able to change him.

"Milky's supposed to be a show horse," Carole continued. "Remember? You said he'd been in lots of shows."

"For years," Lisa said, nodding. "Max told me."

"So we have to assume that he's fully trained," Carole said. "He should understand what Lisa wants him to do, and he should know how he's supposed to behave. It sounds like he doesn't *want* to behave."

"I wish I could make him want to," Lisa said. "I really tried."

"But maybe you can't do it," Carole said. "Maybe no one can. Maybe there's really something wrong with him—some physical thing like a pinched nerve that makes him mean. Maybe despite all his training he's still not a reliable horse."

"I think he just has a personality fault," Stevie said. "He should be agreeable, but he isn't."

"I wonder why not," Lisa said.

"Who knows?" Stevie said. "Maybe something happened to him when he was a foal. Maybe the first people who trained him were cruel to him, so he grew up hating people. Or maybe there's just something wrong with him. Anyway, it's not your fault, and it's certainly not your problem."

Lisa wiped at her eyes again. "I still feel like it is," she said. "I can't help it. If he was going to be my horse—"

"Do you want him?" Stevie asked.

"No, but—"

"Look," Carole said firmly. "You told us that Milky reared with you. Right?"

"Right."

"You have no business riding a horse that rears. None of us does. He could have killed you, Lisa. There's no point in riding a horse like that, not when there are so many good horses around. You should be glad you don't own him yet. You don't have to worry about trying to sell him—you can just tell Max you don't want to ride him anymore."

Lisa blushed. "I haven't told Max about any of our problems," she said.

"Well, you'll have to tell him something."

"I know."

Prancer took a step forward and nosed Lisa's knee. Lisa stroked the mare's forehead. "Remember all the trouble I was having with Prancer last week? She was so frustrating, but she never scared me. I never thought she wanted to hurt me. That's how I felt with Milky, all the time."

"You should have told us," Carole said softly.

"I tried to," Lisa said. "But I didn't really understand how bad he is. Plus, I want my own horse so badly. Part of me still hates to give him up."

"There will be other horses," Carole said.

"I guess so. I never know how my parents are going to act."

"We made a mistake anyway thinking that your problem with Milky and Carole's problem with French were anything alike," Stevie realized. "We should have understood better."

"I don't see how you could have, when I didn't understand myself." Lisa stood up and brushed the hay off her pants. "I'm so glad I talked to you guys. I feel better than I have all week."

"Good," said Stevie. She stood, too. "Let's get our horses and ride while there's still time. I bet Max will let you have Prancer. She can't be in heat anymore, so she'll probably behave."

Lisa grimaced. "First I have to go explain to Max that I'm not really sick— Hey! Where do you think you're going?"

"Outside the stall," Stevie said, confused.

"No—" Lisa pushed past her friend. In the aisle, a small boy named David was walking by leading Milky, who was fully tacked! "What are you doing?" Lisa demanded. David was a little kid—a beginner! He had no business riding Milky!

David frowned. "What do you mean, what am I doing? I'm going to take a riding lesson." He clucked to Milky.

Lisa blocked his way. "You can't ride this horse," she said.

David tried to sidestep her. Milky pranced nervously. "Of course I can," David said. "Max said. He said you hadn't ridden him very hard."

Lisa was appalled. She didn't believe for one minute that Milky would behave better with David than he had with her. He could be killed!

I could have been killed, she realized. The thought shook her like a thunderbolt. *I don't have any business riding Milky. None of us does.* Suddenly she didn't feel guilty anymore.

"You can't ride him," she repeated firmly. "He's dangerous. Give him to me."

"No," David said. He pulled Milky closer to him, a stubborn expression on his face. "I asked Max if I could ride him today, and Max said yes. You've been hogging him all week. He's not your horse."

"That doesn't matter!" Lisa grabbed for Milky's head, but David dodged her. Stevie and Carole came out of Prancer's stall. Stevie caught hold of the stirrup on Milky's saddle, but Milky kicked out. Stevie jumped back, letting go.

"Stop it!" David yelled at them. "I'm telling Max!" He stamped his foot. Milky cocked his hind foot, ready to kick again. Stevie and Carole held back.

"No," Lisa said. "I'll tell Max. You wait here." She ran for the office.

David turned his head and stuck his tongue out at Stevie and Carole. "You're not the bosses of the whole entire stable," he said. "You don't get to tell me what to do." He pulled Milky out the front door.

"Oh, geez," Stevie said. They hurried after him.

"MAX!" LISA BURST into the office. "David's about to ride Milky, and you've got to stop him!"

Max was talking on the telephone. He raised his eyebrows at Lisa and held up one finger, a sign that he didn't want to be disturbed.

"You have to stop him before he gets on," Lisa persisted. "Milky's dangerous! I should have said something—" She glanced out the office window. Carole and Stevie were arguing with David, who had managed to keep hold of Milky's reins and had climbed onto the mounting block. Milky had his ears back in a way Lisa had seen too many times before. And David already had one foot in the stirrup.

"Now!" Lisa shouted. She slammed her hand down on the disconnect button of the phone. Max looked at her in astonishment. Lisa grabbed his arm and pulled him out the office door.

"Lisa, what's going on?" he demanded. Lisa hurried him along the stable aisle.

"You have to stop him!" she pleaded. "Don't let him get hurt!"

"I have to stop who?"

Lisa dropped Max's arm and ran out the main door, toward Milky and David. "Don't!" she cried.

But it was too late. David swung his leg across Milky's back. And Milky reared.

11

WITHOUT THINKING, LISA threw herself forward and grabbed for the reins. Milky's hooves slashed the air dangerously near her head, and she felt one of his forefeet graze her shoulder before she managed to reach one of the reins and momentarily yank his head down. Carole grabbed David as he tumbled off to one side. Milky fought for his head. Lisa hung on desperately while Carole pulled David out of harm's way. Milky reared again. Lisa felt her feet being lifted off the ground.

"Stand clear!" bellowed Max. Lisa let go. Milky's head snapped back when she released it. She watched in horror as he reared higher . . . higher . . . and then one of his hind feet slipped in the dirt. Milky crashed backward, hooves flailing, landing with all his weight on the empty saddle. He scrambled to his feet, shook himself, and went still, looking absolutely unconcerned.

The Saddle Club and Max stood in horrified silence. David sobbed in Carole's arms. On Milky's back, the saddle was twisted and broken.

Max stepped forward and took Milky's reins. He turned to Lisa. "How did you know he was going to do that?" he asked.

"It was her fault," sobbed David. "She yelled at me. She frightened him."

"No," said Max. "She might have yelled, but she didn't frighten him. I saw it. The horse was going to rear anyway. Lisa, how did you know?"

Lisa licked her dry lips. She knew she couldn't lie to Max anymore. As it was, her untruthfulness had nearly caused David great harm. "I didn't *know* he was going to do something," she said. "I just thought he might, because of the look he had on his face. He reared with me this afternoon. Twice," she added.

Max's face went white and then red. "And you didn't tell me," Max said in one of the quietest voices Lisa had ever heard him use.

"And I didn't tell you," Lisa said.

"Is this the first time he's acted like this?"

"It's the first day he's reared," she said. "He's done some other stuff before." She hated to have Max upset with her, but she was surprised by how relieved she felt to finally tell him the truth.

"Why don't I take Milky back to his stall?" suggested Stevie.

Max shook his head. "Go get Red," he told her. "Ask him to put Milky away. None of my students is touching him again." Max smiled at David. "You're going to ride Barq in your lesson now," he told the boy cheerfully. "Why don't you go tack him up, and I'll be right out when I've talked to Lisa for a minute."

David nodded. To Lisa's surprise, he turned to her. "I'm sorry I didn't listen to you," he said. "I was mad that Max was letting you ride Milky all the time. I've been wanting and wanting to ride him."

Lisa understood. "He's pretty, isn't he?"

"Yeah," David said. "I don't want to ride him now, though."

"Go get Barq," Max told him. "Lisa—office."

"Can we come, too, Max?" Carole asked. They all knew that Lisa would be in trouble. Carole didn't want her to have to face it alone.

Max smiled at the entire Saddle Club. He put his arm on Lisa's shoulder. "Of course. I want to talk to Lisa, but I'm not holding an inquisition. In fact, I'd like you to listen to what I have to say."

When Stevie came back with Red, the girls followed Max inside and sat down. Max kicked the door shut. "Trouble?" he asked Lisa gently.

"Every single day," Lisa admitted. She told him all about Milky's behavior. The more she talked, the more agitated Max became. Finally he got up and walked around the room. "I think you were right about him try-ing to bite me last weekend," she concluded, "but I just really didn't want to admit it to myself."

"Why not?" Max asked. "Why didn't you tell me about all this sooner?"

"I kept thinking that he wasn't really that bad," Lisa said. She spread her hands in her lap. She could hear for herself how bad Milky's behavior sounded. "I kept think-ing I could change him. I'm sorry, Max. I know I'm wrong now, but I didn't know I was wrong before. I didn't want to admit that I couldn't ride him."

"Rearing is very dangerous," Max said. "I'm sure you could all see that for yourselves. I've never kept a danger-ous horse in my stables, and I never will. I have too great a responsibility toward my students, and there are plenty of horses that do not have problems. Milky was here on trial, I told you that from the beginning. He's going back tomorrow."

Lisa bowed her head. *Good-bye, dream horse.* But to her surprise, she didn't feel disappointed that Milky was leav-ing. She only felt disappointed that Milky was Milky.

Carole gave Lisa a sympathetic half hug. "What's wrong with Milky, Max? I've never met a horse that acted like he does. Usually a horse is either high-strung or it isn't. I've never seen one that could be so calm one min-ute and so mean the next." Carole had known horses at military stables all over the country. She thought she'd seen almost everything.

"He always felt like he was angry that I was riding

101

him," Lisa said. "Whenever he acted up, I felt like he was doing it to get me off him."

Max nodded. "I do know what you mean. Fortunately, horses like him are extremely rare. Probably, Lisa, he really did want to get you off his back. I don't know what makes a horse act like that—whether it's bad training or something wrong with his brain—but I do know that one who does never belongs in my stable, or in any stable where there are inexperienced riders. I hadn't heard that anyone had had these sorts of problems with Milky, or of course I wouldn't have tried him in the first place. But I did know that he's had several previous owners, so I suspected that something about him might not be right. Usually, people hang on to good horses, especially when they're as beautiful as Milky."

Max quit pacing and sat back down. "Sometimes, if a horse with Milky's personality is extremely talented, a professional rider might try to put up with it, in order to capitalize on its talents in the show ring. But even most professionals won't bother. Most of the time, there is no good home for a horse like him."

"So what's going to happen to him?" Stevie asked. It sounded awful, *no good home*. She had seen what could happen to horses who had bad homes. No animal deserved abuse. On the other hand, she had just seen pretty clearly what could happen to people who had horses like Milky—the mangled saddle on his back was not something she'd soon forget. They were lucky they'd gotten David off in time.

"I don't know," Max admitted. "But since I didn't buy him, he's not my problem. He'll go back to the horse dealer who's trying to sell him, and maybe the dealer will find him a suitable home. If no one wants him, he may end up being euthanized."

"But that's horrible!" Carole said.

"Yes, it is," Max said. "But not nearly as horrible as his hurting David, or one of you, or any other person."

"I guess not," Carole said. It was very difficult for her to accept.

"I know not," Max said firmly. "It's a hard truth, but sometimes life is hard. Honestly, horses like this are very, very rare, but I have seen a few before. I would never knowingly allow one of my students on one. I wouldn't ride Milky myself."

Lisa was astonished. "You wouldn't?" She thought Max could ride anything.

"It's not worth it," Max explained.

Lisa blew out her breath. "Then I guess it's not totally my fault that I couldn't fix him."

"It's completely not your fault," Max said. "Did you think it was?"

"Yes," said Lisa.

Max looked solemn. "Is that why you never told me you were having trouble with him? I'm actually fairly angry with you about this, Lisa. You shouldn't have let this go on so long. And you must have lied to me, because I know I specifically asked you how you were doing, several times."

Lisa didn't know how to explain. "It wasn't that I was trying to lie to you," she said. "I wanted him to be right so much that I kept convincing myself he wasn't really that bad. I know I was lying, but I really didn't mean to be— and I was lying to everyone, to Stevie and Carole and even myself, as well as to you."

Max nodded. Lisa was glad to see that he understood. She knew he was right—she should have told him long ago—but she was glad that he knew she hadn't started out trying to deceive him.

"You put yourself in danger," Max said. "You put the rest of us in danger, too."

Lisa squirmed. "I know, and I'm really sorry. But Max, I didn't understand that until today. I didn't know a horse could be like Milky. I really didn't. I thought that if I was patient enough, and good enough, I could always fix any horse."

"I thought so, too," Carole said in a small voice. "I have to admit, Max, whenever Lisa tried to tell us about the problems she was having, Stevie and I encouraged her to try harder or try different things. We didn't tell her to come to you."

"So now you know," Max said. "Listen, and listen hard, because I don't want any of you forgetting this again: You have to tell me when you're having problems with your horses. Even Belle and Starlight. Red and I are always here to help you, but we can't solve problems when we don't know they exist. Okay?"

"Okay," agreed The Saddle Club.

"I'm to blame, too," said Max. "I should have supervised you a little more closely, Lisa. I also realize that Milky's problems were beyond your experience. You can't be expected to deal with something you've never even heard about before. But part of this is your fault. You should have told me, and I am going to have to punish you."

"Okay." Lisa bowed her head. She knew she deserved something, but she hoped Max wasn't going to expel her from the barn for the semester. She hoped he didn't say she could never ride Prancer again.

"You're grounded for a week," Max said. "No riding. I'll still expect you here for your lesson and for Pony Club, but you won't ride. You'll stand on the sidelines and watch and learn. Next Friday you can ride again."

Lisa knew that he was being more than fair. She tried to smile at him, but the smile wavered a little. Max smiled back. "Get out of here," he told them, waving his hand toward the door. "Go groom your horses. The lecture's over."

"Am I still allowed to groom?" Lisa asked.

Max laughed. "Yes. You're also allowed to clean tack and muck stalls."

"WELL," STEVIE SAID as they headed for the tack room, "that really wasn't so bad. I mean, I know it stinks for you, Lisa, but—"

"But it could have been a lot worse," Lisa agreed. "No, I think Max is being fair. I still have the worst part left to come, though." She sat down on a tack trunk and leaned against the wall.

Carole sat down next to her. "He's definitely not your dream horse, is he?" she said sympathetically.

"Nope," said Lisa. "And now I've got to go home and explain to my parents that I don't want Milky."

"Mom?" Lisa CROSSED the living room nervously and stood in front of her parents, wringing her hands. "Dad? Can I talk to you about something? It's important."

Her parents looked at each other. Lisa's father put down the book he was reading. Her mother clicked off the television. "Of course, dear." Her mother patted the empty sofa cushion beside her. "Come, sit down."

Lisa sat. She was glad she had the chance to speak to both her parents at once, and glad they were both listening, but she still didn't feel very comfortable. "Keep it simple," Carole had said. Lisa knew that was good advice: Her parents didn't understand horses. They would never really understand Milky, and Lisa didn't want to scare them away from buying her a different horse.

"Milky and I just aren't getting along," she began.
Lisa's mother looked puzzled. "You're not?"

"No," Lisa said. "He's just—His personality is—He's really very difficult. I've been trying hard and spending a lot of time with him this week, but we're really not developing a good relationship. In fact, I'm not sure I could say we've developed any relationship at all."

Mr. Atwood nodded. He looked serious. "No relationship," he said. "I see. And . . . this is a problem?"

"Well, of course," Lisa said. "It's essential. I mean, how could we be together otherwise? But he doesn't want to try. He doesn't want to do what I ask him to do."

Her parents exchanged glances. "Maybe you're expecting too much of him," Mrs. Atwood suggested. "Did you really spend the whole week together?"

"Well, of course," Lisa said. "I felt like I had to."

"I don't think you should be telling him what to do," Mrs. Atwood said.

"At your age," cut in Mr. Atwood. "No need to rush."

"Maybe you're moving too fast," suggested Mrs. Atwood.

"Max doesn't think so," said Lisa.

Mrs. Atwood looked startled. "You've discussed this with Max?"

"Yes," Lisa said. "I didn't think you'd mind."

"Well, no, I suppose not." Mr. Atwood was also looking a little ruffled. "What did Max advise?"

"He feels the same way I do." Lisa pulled herself up straighter and took a deep breath. "Mom, Dad, it's hard for me to tell you this, but neither Max nor I think that Milky's a good horse for me."

Her parents looked at each other and burst out laughing. Lisa felt exceptionally annoyed. After all she'd been through that week, they thought it was funny?

"Milky is a horse!" said Lisa's mother.

"Well, of course," Lisa said. "What did you think he was, a pony?"

"A boy," her mother said, between chuckles. "We thought he was a boy. From your school. A crush, maybe."

"*A boy named Milky?*"

Mr. Atwood shrugged. "They all have such weird names these days. Besides, when I was a boy, I had a friend we called Cheese. Milky's not too far a stretch."

"Why would I be spending all my time with a boy?" Lisa asked. She liked being around boys—some of them— but really, it sounded like a waste of a week.

"I don't know," her mother said, more seriously now. "We're glad you're not. You had us worried for a moment there. So, what's the problem with this horse?"

Lisa realized that her parents might not be recognizing the nickname Milky. "It's Au Lait," she said. "The Thoroughbred? Remember?"

"I don't see what the problem is," her father said. "If you're not getting along with him, ride a different horse. Max has got a stableful, hasn't he? Is he trying to make you ride this one?"

"No," Lisa said. She finally realized that her parents

really didn't know what she was talking about. "I thought you were—I mean—I thought you wanted to buy him for me."

Lisa's father shook his head. "Max lets you ride whenever you want," he said. "Why would we go to all the trouble of getting you one?"

"Sweetie." Lisa's mother reached for her hand. "Why did you think we were getting you a horse?"

Lisa didn't know whether to laugh or cry. So this whole horrible week had been for nothing! Suddenly it did strike her as funny, sort of. She shook her head. "I heard you talking to Max on the phone," she told her mother. "I didn't mean to hear, but I did. You were asking him if something had arrived, and it sounded like you meant it to be a secret, and that was the afternoon that Milky arrived at the barn. So I thought he was the secret."

Mrs. Atwood patted Lisa's hand. "I'm sorry to disappoint you, dear, though I guess you can't be too disappointed if you don't like the horse anyway."

"I guess not," Lisa said.

Her mother grinned. "I'll tell you what the secret is, even though it's still not ready. You'll love it! I've ordered you a new show jacket. Max said you'd probably be riding in some competitions early next year, so I got him to help me pick out exactly the right kind of jacket—you know, a good brand, well made, the right style. Max said navy blue pinstripes are considered very correct right now, and I thought that would contrast beautifully with Prancer's red fur. Max ordered it from a catalog, but it hasn't come in yet. Won't that be wonderful?"

"Sure." Lisa felt a little bewildered. Trust her mother to think of horses in terms of clothes! Still, it was very sweet of her to buy Lisa a new coat and to go to so much trouble to be sure it was a good one. "I bet it'll be a super coat," she said. "Thank you."

"We want the best for you, Lisa," said her father. He picked his book back off the floor.

"Weren't you . . . Weren't you thinking about getting me a horse at all? You wanted to that one time."

Her parents looked at her quizzically. "Now that we know more about horses, it seems like a lot of bother," said her father. "Doesn't Max let you ride whenever you want?"

"Yes, but—"

"Don't you love riding Prancer?" asked Lisa's mother.

"Yes, but—" Lisa shook her head. Maybe someday she'd talk them into changing their minds again. Meanwhile, she could ride Prancer almost any time she wanted. "Yes," she agreed. "I do."

"SO, DID THEY understand?" Stevie asked eagerly. They'd made Lisa promise that she'd call them right after she talked with her parents.

"Not at all," Lisa said. "They thought Milky was a boy, and they didn't understand why I was worried about our relationship. I think for a few minutes they were pretty worried about me. But it doesn't matter, because they were planning on buying me a show coat, not a horse."

"A show coat?" asked Carole.

"Pretty hard to ride one of those," commented Stevie. "Though I guess it wouldn't rear or try to buck you off."

"Don't remind me," Lisa said. "I'd like to forget this week. The worst part is, my parents aren't even close to getting me my own horse."

"We're so sorry," Carole said. "I never really thought that you and Milky were a great match, but I did want you to have a horse of your own."

"Me too," said Stevie. "But don't give up hope. I never thought my parents were going to let me get a horse, and then all of a sudden, I got Belle. So it could happen."

"I'll keep my fingers crossed."

"We're glad you're back to normal," Stevie said. "I mean, not worried about Milky."

"I wouldn't call it normal yet," Lisa said. "Next week, when I'm riding again, that might be normal."

"Hey, I've got to go," Carole said. "Sorry, but Dad invited dinner guests, and they just got here. I'm going to make them listen to my latest French dialogue." She hung up.

"I'm glad The Saddle Club could help Carole, anyway," Stevie told Lisa. "I'm sorry that we couldn't be more helpful to you."

"Don't be." Lisa twirled the phone cord between her fingertips. She looked out her bedroom window at the rising moon. "I don't think anyone could really help me. I was never going to make Milky into the horse of my dreams."

"I know," said Stevie. "I'm still sorry." They said goodbye and disconnected. Lisa walked over to her window and pressed her face against the glass. Somewhere out there the horse of her dreams was waiting. Someday she would have a horse of her own.

13

"HOW DOES IT feel?" Carole asked.

"Wonderful!" Lisa's face glowed with happiness. It was Friday afternoon, a crisp, clear, cloudless day. Her punishment was over: Lisa was riding Prancer at a brisk trot, and The Saddle Club was out on the trails once again.

" 'Back in the saddle again,' " sang Stevie, " 'Oh, back in the saddle again—' "

"It was nice of you guys to give up trail riding for this last week," Lisa said. "You didn't have to, but it did make it easier on me. Watching you ride in the ring without me was agony enough."

"It's never as much fun unless we're all together," Stevie said. "When you're not with us because of piano or ballet, that's one thing, but when you are at the stable

114

and you're just not allowed on a horse, Carole and I would feel pretty rude if we abandoned you."

"All for one and one for all," Carole said. She felt as high-spirited as the rest of them. That day, her dialogue in French had received a solid B, and her teacher had commented on how much she'd improved. "We're a team."

"No, a club," said Stevie.

"The Saddle Club!" Lisa waved her riding crop like a flag. Prancer began to prance nervously. Lisa put her crop back down and patted the mare. "Sorry, dear. I wasn't going to hit you."

"You and Prancer look like a team again," Stevie said. Lisa laughed. "Well, for one thing, she's no longer in heat. But I think I'll never again get quite as frustrated with her as I did before I met Milky. Compared to him, Prancer is a piece of cake."

"Almost any horse is." Carole slowed Starlight to a sober walk. "Did you ask Max what happened to him?" Milky had left Pine Hollow the night Lisa confessed everything to Max. Carole knew they'd never see the gray horse again. It wasn't that she wanted to, but still . . .

Lisa slowed Prancer to match Starlight's stride. Stevie rode Belle up along Starlight's other side. "I did ask him," Lisa confirmed. "Max said we'll never know, because he's never going to ask. He said Milky is the horse dealer's business, not ours."

Stevie whistled. "That's harsh."

"Not really." Carole shook her head and sighed. "You

know, before last week, if you had asked me, I would have said any horse could be retrained out of its problems. I really thought that was true. And I would have said Max could ride any horse in the world."

"But Max said he wouldn't ride Milky," Lisa remembered.

"That's right," Carole said. "I guess I know now that there are some horses that can never be trusted. I spent some time last night looking up training issues in some of my riding books and magazines, and I was amazed by what some of the professional riders said."

"Like what?" Lisa wanted to hear it. She still felt a tiny bit guilty about Milky.

"Well, for one, almost all of them think that a horse's temperament is the most important thing about it. They say you can train a horse to be afraid of something, for instance, but you can't train it to be naturally brave. And you can't train it to try hard."

"To have heart," Stevie interpreted, "like our horses do."

Carole nodded. "That's right. And they all said that some horses should be avoided at all costs—ones that kick or bite or rear. Take rearing, for instance—"

"Yes, please take it," Lisa joked. "I never want that to happen to me again."

"If a horse falls over backward, the way Milky did, it can get hurt," Carole said. "Horses know this. So if a horse rears not because something startled him but because he wants you off his back, then he's actually willing to hurt himself in order to hurt you."

Stevie and Lisa digested this. "That's a pretty powerful statement," Lisa said.

Carole looked grim. "One book said, flat out, 'Horses who rear should be shot.' That's how dangerous the writer thought they were."

Stevie shook her head. "Who wrote the book? Some crackpot?"

"No," said Carole. "A former Olympic show jumper known for how well he dealt with difficult horses."

"Wow," Lisa said.

"And I read a Bruce Davidson column in an old issue of *HorsePlay* magazine about how to choose a horse," Carole continued.

Stevie grinned. "What did he say? If anyone can deal with temperamental horses, Bruce Davidson can." Bruce Davidson was an event rider who'd been to the Olympics five times. Stevie had a giant poster of him on her wall; he was one of her heroes.

"He said he doesn't have time to deal with neurotic horses," Carole said. "He won't buy them."

"Gosh." Stevie was impressed. So was Lisa. The last flicker of her guilt over Milky disappeared. If Max and Bruce Davidson wouldn't ride him, then clearly she couldn't be blamed for not wanting to, either.

Lisa suggested that they trot again. The week she'd spent grounded had gone fairly quickly, since Max hadn't banned her from the stables and there was always plenty of work to do, but she loved being back on Prancer again. She sent the mare forward into the wind.

"I never knew horses like Milky even existed," she said. She had to speak more loudly now that they were moving faster. "It's so sad that they do. But it would have been even sadder if David had been hurt."

"Or you," Stevie said firmly.

"I guess that shows how lucky we are, not to have ever known a bad horse before," Carole commented. "Max does such a good job finding horses for Pine Hollow."

"Yes, he does, but probably it also shows just how few bad horses there really are," Stevie said.

"I hope so," said Lisa. "And someday I am getting a horse of my own, even if I have to wait until I can buy it myself."

"Of course," said Carole. "And when you do, it won't be like Milky."

Lisa looked down at Prancer's silky black mane. "No, it won't be. Hey, let's gallop!" They'd reached an open field.

Carole held up her hand. "Wait just a minute. First I want to recite some French."

Stevie suppressed a moan. "I didn't think your next dialogue was due until Wednesday!"

"This isn't part of a dialogue—well, it is, but it's a line from an old one that I've adapted. My French teacher told me the word for *horse*."

Carole stood in her stirrups and waved her hand with a flourish. "*Ces chevaux*," she intoned, "*sont magnifiques!*"

She sat back in the saddle and signaled to Starlight. He shot forward over the grass.

Stevie and Lisa galloped after her. "What does that mean?" Lisa shouted.

Carole laughed. " 'These horses are magnificent!' "

What happens to The Saddle Club next?
Read Bonnie Bryant's exciting new series
and find out.

High school. Driver's licenses. Boyfriends. Jobs.

A lot of new things are happening, but one thing remains the same: Stevie Lake, Lisa Atwood, and Carole Hanson are still best friends. However, even among best friends some things do change, and problems can strain any friendship . . . but these three can handle it. Can't they?

Read an excerpt from Pine Hollow #1: *The Long Ride*.

PROLOGUE

"DO YOU THINK we'll get there in time?" Stevie Lake asked, looking around for some reassuring sign that the airport was near.

"Since that plane almost landed on us, I think it's safe to say that we're close," Carole Hanson said.

"Turn right here," said Callie Forester from the backseat.

"And then left up ahead," Carole advised, picking out directions from the signs that flashed past near the airport entrance. "I think Lisa's plane is leaving from that terminal there."

"Which one?"

"The one we just passed," Callie said.

"Oh," said Stevie. She gripped the steering wheel tightly and looked for a way to turn around without causing a major traffic tie-up.

"This would be easier if we were on horseback," said Carole.

"Everything's easier on horseback," Stevie agreed.

"Or if we had a police escort," said Callie.

"Have you done that?" Stevie asked, trying to maneuver the car across three lanes of traffic.

"I have," said Callie. "It's kind of fun, but dangerous. It makes you think you're almost as important as other people tell you you are."

Stevie rolled her window down and waved wildly at the confused drivers around her. Clearly, her waving confused them more, but it worked. All traffic stopped. She crossed the necessary three lanes and pulled onto the service road.

It took another ten minutes to get back to the right and then ten more to find a parking place. Five minutes into the terminal. And then all that was left was to find Lisa.

"Where do you think she is?" Carole asked.

"I know," said Stevie. "Follow me."

"That's what we've been doing all morning," Callie said dryly. "And look how far it's gotten us."

But she followed anyway.

ALEX LAKE REACHED across the table in the airport cafeteria and took Lisa Atwood's hand.

"It's going to be a long summer," he said.

Lisa nodded. Saying good-bye was one of her least favorite activities. She didn't want Alex to know how hard it was, though. That would just make it tougher on him. The two of them had known each other for four years—as long as Lisa had been best friends with Alex's twin sister, Stevie. But they'd only started dating six months earlier. Lisa could hardly believe that. It seemed as if she'd been in love with him forever.

"But it is just for the summer," she said. The words sounded dumb even as they came out of her mouth. The summer *was* long. She wouldn't come back to Virginia until right before school started.

"I wish your dad didn't live so far away, and I wish the summer weren't so long."

"It'll go fast," said Lisa.

"For you, maybe. You'll be in California, surfing or some-thing. I'll just be here, mowing lawns."

"I've never surfed in my life—"

"Until now," said Alex. It was almost a challenge, and Lisa didn't like it.

"I don't want to fight with you," said Lisa.

"I don't want to fight with you, either," he said, re-lenting. "I'm sorry. It's just that I want things to be different. Not very different. Just a little different."

"Me too," said Lisa. She squeezed his hand. It was a way to keep from saying anything else, because she was afraid that if she tried to speak she might cry, and she hated it when she cried. It made her face red and puffy, but most of all, it told other people how she was feeling. She'd found it useful to keep her feelings to herself these days. Like Alex, she wanted things to be different, but she wanted them to be very different, not just a little. She sighed. That was slightly better than crying.

"I TOLD YOU SO," said Stevie to Callie and Carole.

Stevie had threaded her way through the airport termi-nal, straight to the cafeteria near the security checkpoint. And there, sitting next to the door, were her twin brother and her best friend.

"Surprise!" the three girls cried, crowding around the table.

"We just couldn't let you be the only one to say good-bye to Lisa," Carole said, sliding into the booth next to Alex.

"We had to be here, too. You understand that, don't you?" Stevie asked Lisa as she sat down next to her.

"And since I was in the car, they brought me along," said Callie, pulling up a chair from a nearby table.

"You guys!" said Lisa, her face lighting up with joy. "I'm so glad you're here. I was afraid I wasn't going to see you for months and months!"

She *was* glad they were there. It wouldn't have felt right if she'd had to leave without seeing them one more time. "I thought you had other things to do."

"We just told you that so we could surprise you. We did surprise you, didn't we?"

"You surprised me," Lisa said, beaming.

"Me too," Alex said dryly. "I'm surprised, too. I really thought I could go for an afternoon, just *one* afternoon of my life, without seeing my twin sister."

Stevie grinned. "Well, there's always tomorrow," she said. "And that's something to look forward to, right?"

"Right," he said, grinning back.

Since she was closest to the outside, Callie went and got sodas for herself, Stevie, and Carole. When she rejoined the group, they were talking about everything in the world except the fact that Lisa was going to be gone for the summer and how much they were all going to miss one another.

She passed the drinks around and sat quietly at the end of the table. There wasn't much for her to say. She didn't really feel as if she belonged there. She wasn't anybody's best friend. It wasn't as if they minded her being there, but she'd come along because Stevie had offered to drive her to a tack shop after they left the airport. She was simply along for the ride.

". . . And don't forget to say hello to Skye."

"Skye? Skye who?" asked Alex.

"Don't pay any attention to him," Lisa said. "He's just jealous."

"You mean because Skye is a movie star?"

"And say hi to your father and the new baby. It must be exciting that you'll meet your sister."

"Well, of course, you've already met her, but now she's crawling, right? It's a whole different thing."

An announcement over the PA system brought their chatter to a sudden halt.

"It's my flight," Lisa said slowly. "They're starting to board and I've got to get through security and then to Gate . . . whatever."

"Fourteen," Alex said. "It comes after Gate Twelve. There are no thirteens in airports."

"Let's go."

"Here, I'll carry that."

"And I'll get this one . . ."

As Callie watched, Lisa hugged Carole and Stevie. Then she kissed Alex. Then she hugged her friends again. Then she turned to Alex.

"I think it's time for us to go," Carole said tactfully.

"Write or call every day," Stevie said.

"It's a promise," said Lisa. "Thanks for coming to the airport. You, too, Callie."

Callie smiled and gave Lisa a quick hug before all the girls backed off from Lisa and Alex.

Lisa waved. Her friends waved and turned to leave her alone with Alex. They were all going to miss her, but the girls had one another. Alex only had his lawns to mow. He needed the last minutes with Lisa.

"See you at home!" Stevie called over her shoulder, but she didn't think Alex heard. His attention was completely focused on one person.

Carole wiped a tear from her eye once they'd rounded a corner. "I'm going to miss her."

"Me too," said Stevie.

Carole turned to Callie. "It must be hard for you to understand," she said.

"Not really," said Callie. "I can tell you three are really close."

"We are," Carole said. "Best friends for a long time. We're practically inseparable." Even to her the words sounded exclusive and uninviting. If Callie noticed, she didn't say anything.

The three girls walked out of the terminal and found their way to Stevie's car. As she turned on the engine, Stevie was aware of an uncomfortable empty feeling. She really didn't like the idea of Lisa's being gone for the summer, and her own unhappiness was not going to be helped by a brother who was going to spend the entire time moping about his missing girlfriend. There had to be something that would make her feel better.

"Say, Carole, do you want to come along with us to the tack shop?" she asked.

"No, I can't," Carole said. "I promised I'd bring in the horses from the paddock before dark, so you can just drop me off at Pine Hollow. Anyway, aren't you due at work in an hour?"

Stevie glanced at her watch. Carole was right. Everything was taking longer than it was supposed to this afternoon.

"Don't worry," Callie said quickly. "We can go to the tack shop another time."

"You don't mind?" Stevie asked.

"No. I don't. Really," said Callie. "I don't want you to be late for work—either of you. If my parents decide to get a pizza for dinner again, I'm going to want it to arrive on time!"

Stevie laughed, but not because she thought anything was very funny. She wasn't about to forget the last time she'd delivered a pizza to Callie's family. In fact, she wished it hadn't happened, but it had. Now she had to find a way to face up to it.

As she pulled out of the airport parking lot, a plane roared overhead, rising into the brooding sky. *Maybe that's Lisa's plane*, she thought. The noise of its flight seemed to mark the beginning of a long summer.

The first splats of rain hit the windshield as Stevie paid their way out of the parking lot. By the time they were on the highway, it was raining hard. The sky had darkened to a steely gray. Streaks of lightning brightened it, only to be followed by thunder that made the girls jump.

The storm had come out of nowhere. Stevie flicked on the windshield wipers and hoped it would go right back to nowhere.

The sky turned almost black as the storm strengthened. Curtains of rain ripped across the windshield, pounding on the hood and roof of the car. The wipers flicked uselessly at the torrent.

"I hope Fez is okay," said Callie. "He hates thunder, you know."

"I'm not surprised," said Carole, trying to control her

voice. It seemed to her that there were a lot of things Fez hated. He was as temperamental as any horse she had ever ridden.

Fez was one of the horses in the paddock. Carole didn't want to upset Callie by telling her that. If she told Callie he'd been turned out, Callie would wonder why he hadn't just been exercised. If she told Callie she'd exercised him, Callie might wonder if he was being overworked. Carole shook her head. What was it about this girl that made Carole so certain that whatever she said, it would be wrong? Why couldn't she say the one thing she really needed to say?

Still, Carole worked at Pine Hollow, and that meant taking care of the horses that were boarding there—and that meant keeping the owners happy.

"I'm sure Fez will be fine. Ben and Max will look after him," Carole said.

"I guess you're right," said Callie. "I know he can be difficult. Of course, you've ridden him, so you know that, too. I mean, that's obvious. But it's spirit, you see. Spirit is the key to an endurance specialist. He's got it, and I think he's got the makings of a champion. We'll work together this summer, and come fall . . . well, you'll see."

Spirit—yes, it was important in a horse. Carole knew that. She just wished she understood why it was that Fez's spirit was so irritating to her. She'd always thought of herself as someone who'd never met a horse she didn't like. Maybe it was the horse's owner . . .

"Uh-oh," said Stevie, putting her foot gently on the brake. "I think I got it going a little too fast there."

"You've got to watch out for that," Callie said. "My

father says the police practically lie in wait for teenage drivers. They love to give us tickets. Well, they certainly had fun with me."

"You got a ticket?" Stevie asked.

"No, I just got a warning, but it was almost worse than a ticket. I was going four miles over the speed limit in our hometown. The policeman stopped me, and when he saw who I was, he just gave me a warning. Dad was furious—at me and at the officer, though he didn't say anything to the officer. He was angry at him because he thought someone would find out and say I'd gotten special treatment! I was only going four miles over the speed limit. Really. Even the officer said that. Well, it would have been easier if I'd gotten a ticket. Instead, I got grounded. Dad won't let me drive for three months. Of course, that's nothing compared to what happened to Scott last year."

"What happened to Scott?" Carole asked, suddenly curious about the driving challenges of the Forester children.

"Well, it's kind of a long story," said Callie. "But—"

"Wow! Look at that!" Stevie interrupted. There was an amazing streak of lightning over the road ahead. The dark afternoon brightened for a minute. Thunder followed instantly.

"Maybe we should pull off the road or something?" Carole suggested.

"I don't think so," said Stevie. She squinted through the windshield. "It's not going to last long. It never does when it rains this hard. We get off at the next exit anyway."

She slowed down some more and turned the wipers up a notch. She followed the car in front of her, keeping a constant eye on the two red spots of the car's taillights. She'd be okay as long as she could see them. The rain pelted the car so loudly that it was hard to talk. Stevie drove on cautiously.

Then, as suddenly as it had started, the rain stopped. Stevie spotted the sign for their exit, signaled, and pulled off to the right and up the ramp. She took a left onto the overpass and followed the road toward Willow Creek.

The sky was as dark as it had been, and there were clues that there had been some rain there, but nothing nearly as hard as the rain they'd left on the interstate. Stevie sighed with relief and switched the windshield wipers to a slower rate.

"I think I'll drop you off at Pine Hollow first," she said, turning onto the road that bordered the stable's property.

Pine Hollow's white fences followed the contour of the road, breaking the open, grassy hillside into a sequence of paddocks and fields. A few horses stood in the fields, swishing their tails. One bucked playfully and ran up a hill, shaking his head to free his mane in the wind. Stevie smiled. Horses always seemed to her the most welcoming sight in the world.

"Then I'll take Callie home," Stevie continued, "and after that I'll go over to Pizza Manor. I may be a few minutes late for work, but who orders pizza at five o'clock in the afternoon anyway?"

"Now, now," teased Carole. "Is that any way for you to mind your Pizza Manors?"

"Well, at least I have my hat with me," said Stevie. Or did she? She looked into the rearview mirror to see if she could spot it, and when that didn't do any good, she glanced over her shoulder. Callie picked it up and started to hand it to her.

"Here," she said. "We wouldn't want— Wow! I guess the storm isn't over yet!"

The sky had suddenly filled with a brilliant streak of lightning, jagged and pulsating, accompanied by an explosion of thunder.

It startled Stevie. She shrieked and turned her face back to the road. The light was so sudden and so bright that it blinded her for a second. The car swerved. Stevie braked. She clutched at the steering wheel and then realized she couldn't see because the rain was pelting even harder than before. She reached for the wiper control, switching it to its fastest speed.

There was something to her right! She saw something move, but she didn't know what it was.

"Stevie!" Carole cried.

"Look out!" Callie screamed from the backseat.

Stevie swerved to the left on the narrow road, hoping it would be enough. Her answer was a sickening jolt as the car slammed into something solid. The car spun around, smashing against the thing again. When the thing screamed, Stevie knew it was a horse. Then it disappeared from her field of vision. Once again, the car spun. It smashed against the guardrail on the left side of the road and tumbled up and over it as if the rail had never been there.

Down they went, rolling, spinning. Stevie could hear the screams of her friends. She could hear her own voice, echoing in the close confines of the car, answered by the thumps of the car rolling down the hillside into a gully. Suddenly the thumping stopped. The screams were stilled. The engine cut off. The wheels stopped spinning. And all Stevie could hear was the idle *slap, slap, slap* of her windshield wipers.

"Carole?" she whispered. "Are you okay?"

"I think so. What about you?" Carole answered.

"Me too. Callie? Are you okay?" Stevie asked.

There was no answer.

"Callie?" Carole echoed.

The only response was the girl's shallow breathing.

How could this have happened?

ABOUT THE AUTHOR

Bonnie Bryant is the author of nearly a hundred books about horses, including The Saddle Club series, Saddle Club Super Editions, and the Pony Tails series. She has also written novels and movie novelizations under her married name, B. B. Hiller.

Ms. Bryant began writing The Saddle Club in 1986. Although she had done some riding before that, she intensified her studies then and found herself learning right along with her characters Stevie, Carole, and Lisa. She claims that they are all much better riders than she is.

Ms. Bryant was born and raised in New York City. She still lives there, in Greenwich Village, with her two sons.

Don't miss the next exciting
Saddle Club adventure . . .

CHRISTMAS TREASURE
Saddle Club Super #7

Christmas is coming, and Max wants Horse Wise to get
into the holiday spirit. He announces that they're going
to have Secret Santas, but there's a catch: They can't
give something; they have to *do* something. It sounds
like fun—until they draw names. Lisa gets Max. Carole
gets Lisa. And Stevie gets Veronica.

Carole wants to come up with the perfect good deed
for Lisa, but since they're always doing things for each
other anyway, what can she do that's really special? As
for Lisa, her visiting relatives aren't giving her room to
breathe—there's no time to do anything for Max. And
Stevie would love to do something *to* Veronica, but that
wouldn't be in the holiday spirit.

If the perfect Christmas gift doesn't come wrapped up
in paper and tied with ribbon . . . what is it?